CW00410247

FALLING FOR HER BODYGUARD

BODYGUARD SERIES BOOK 2

EMILY HAYES

1

MORGAN

Morgan Hart sighed as she leaned back in the bath. She needed this. Her last job had been long and tedious. Guarding the son of a high-ranking politician sounded pretty glamorous until you realized that his father was only hiring a bodyguard to make himself and his family look more impressive to the press rather than because of any actual danger.

So, Morgan had been stuck going to polo tournaments with Josh and hanging out with him and his dumb friends, who wouldn't stop hitting on her, despite knowing very well that she was gay. She had dearly wanted to quit, but she was a new hire in Gray's company and she didn't want to make a bad impression by quitting the third job she'd been assigned to.

So, she'd stuck it out. Eventually, Josh's father had realized that having a bodyguard when his family was under no threat was a pointless endeavor—which, Morgan thought sourly, she could have told him from the start.

She breathed in the sweet scent of the rose oil she had put in her bath and sipped on her wine. Hopefully, her next job would offer a bit more excitement and be absent of idiot men hitting on her.

She was just taking another sip of wine when her phone rang. Morgan was sorely tempted to ignore it, but she saw it was Gray. She groaned. She'd told Gray she was ready to take on another job immediately, but she didn't think Gray would get back to her within hours of telling her that.

"Hello?"

"Hi, Morgan. I'm sorry to call you at this time, but I just got word of an urgent job. Are you interested?"

"What's the job?" Morgan asked cautiously. New hire or not, if it was another fake job that was just for show, she was turning it down.

"Ms. Leigh Rayson. She's a thirty-year-old heiress to a family fortune. I think her mother is a bigshot in the oil industry. For the last few months, she's been getting death threats, and the police aren't making any progress on who has it in for her."

Well, that certainly sounded like a real job. "She's been getting death threats for months and she's only contacting a bodyguard company now? I would have thought someone with her money would have done so sooner."

"That's just the thing. I'm not entirely sure what her problem is, but she's been through five different companies in the past three months. She's fired each one of them for what seem to me to be increasingly ridiculous reasons. It's like she doesn't want a bodyguard, but then she goes and hires another one."

That did seem odd. "Well, maybe I'll be the one to win her over."

"This will likely be a difficult job. Working with uncooperative clients can be trying—I know that first hand."

"I can do it." Morgan resolved to stick with it and convince Leigh to let her stay, no matter how difficult Leigh was.

"If you're sure, I'll send you the details."

"Please do. I'll contact her tomorrow to set up a meeting."

"Thanks, Morgan."

"Any time."

Morgan smiled as she hung up the phone. She had felt a little insecure coming to Gray's company. Almost everyone who worked for Gray was ex-military. Morgan was the only one with no form of military or law enforcement training. Of course, with black belts in Karate, Jiu Jitsu, Aikido and Krav Maga, she was more than capable of defending herself and her clients, but she couldn't help but feel the need to prove herself. Martial arts had always been Morgan's passion. Her father was a world renowned expert in Aikido and Morgan had learnt martial arts and self defence from an early age. Unarmed combat was her speciality and it was yet to let her down.

Morgan finished her bath quicker than she'd intended to, curious about the information Gray was sending over. By the time she was dressed, she had an email with half a dozen attachments. Morgan loved how thoroughly Gray always vetted potential clients. The more information Morgan had, the better she was able to do her job.

It seemed that Ms. Leigh Rayson had lived a charmed life up until now. She breezed through school with top grades, though had decided not to take her studies further. Her fiancé, Jake, seemed like an all-round great guy. He and Leigh spent their days attending charity functions and art gallery openings, going shopping, or lazing about their mansion just outside of the city.

Morgan frowned as she read on. Leigh and Jake didn't seem to have any friends. It was odd, because from what Morgan could determine about them, they both seemed like nice people. With Leigh's money, she couldn't exactly be lacking in people wanting to befriend her.

Maybe she was pushing people away because she was afraid they only wanted her for her money? Morgan couldn't think of any other reason for it. She supposed it would make her job easier —it made for a smaller suspect pool.

What she really needed was to catch the person delivering the threats red-handed and turn them over to the police. She'd need to keep a close eye on Leigh and make sure not to let her go anywhere alone. Hopefully, she could catch the person in question before Leigh found some reason to fire her.

Morgan went to bed that night with her mind spinning with possibilities. She wondered what security at Leigh's mansion was like. She'd take a look tomorrow and have Leigh upgrade it if necessary. They'd need cameras and a state-of-the-art alarm system, of course.

She woke early the next day and went to the gym, since it was too early to call Leigh. The last thing Morgan needed was to make a bad impression by waking Leigh up. She didn't need to give Leigh any reasons to fire her, especially since it seemed that Leigh had no problem coming up with increasingly ludicrous reasons on her own.

Her last bodyguard had been fired for folding her dinner napkin incorrectly. Apparently, Leigh's mother had taken offense and there had been a fight about it. As if that was the guard's fault. Anyone who would fight over the way a dinner napkin was folded clearly had too much time on their hands.

Morgan looked around, searching for a training partner. There was always someone at this time of day, wanting to get in some sparring before work.

As she looked, she saw Max come out of the

locker rooms and caught his eye. "Hey, Max, are you free to roll with me?"

"Always for you, Morgan."

She and Max were both soon sweaty and grinning as they grappled for dominance. Morgan won, but only by the slimmest of hairs. She and Max were well-matched.

"Thanks, Max. I may be out for a while—I have a new client, who's probably going to be more demanding than the last one."

"I would hope so. You were bored out of your mind with the last one."

"I really was. This job is going to be much more exciting, I'm sure." If she could convince Leigh to keep her on for long enough to solve this mystery.

Morgan went home and showered. When she was done with breakfast, she decided that Leigh must be up by now. She called Leigh's number, which rang, but there was no answer. Morgan hung up and sent a WhatsApp instead.

Hi Leigh, my name is Morgan. Gray has assigned me to guard you. When are you free to meet? I'm ready to start at once. Please let me know.

.   .   .

Morgan spent the next several hours checking her phone. Leigh read the message less than an hour after Morgan sent it, but she didn't respond. Morgan did her best not to be impatient. Leigh was probably just busy doing whatever heiresses did and hadn't had a chance to respond yet.

She and her fiancé were getting married in six months. Maybe she was busy planning the wedding. Morgan would have thought they'd hire a wedding planner, but perhaps Leigh was the type of person who liked to do things herself.

By lunch time, there was still no response, so Morgan tried calling again. Still no answer. Leigh had been online multiple times since seeing Morgan's message and still showed no sign of responding.

Afternoon stretched into evening and still nothing from Leigh. Morgan decided to send another WhatsApp.

Hey, Leigh, it's Morgan again. Just checking in if you're still interested in having someone from our company guard you. No worries if you've changed your mind – just let me know. If you are still interested in our services, I'd like to get started as soon as possible. I've read the threats against you and they sound serious. I'd like to ensure your safety as quickly as I can.

Still nothing. Morgan navigated to Gray's WhatsApp.

Do you know if Leigh still wants a bodyguard? I've tried to contact her multiple times, but she's not responding.

Gray, at least, replied quickly.

She hasn't said anything to me about changing her mind. I'll see if I can get hold of her.

Thanks, Gray. Let me know what she says.

Will do.

. . .

The next morning, Morgan woke up to a message from Gray.

Leigh says she still wants a bodyguard. I asked her if she got your messages, and she said she hasn't had a chance to respond yet and will do so when she can.

Morgan wondered why Leigh had time to respond to Gray's messages and not hers. She suspected that Leigh was getting cold feet. The woman was clearly torn over whether she even wanted someone guarding her. The fact that she kept firing her guards spoke to her desperately wanting to be left alone, but she took the threat to her life seriously enough to keep hiring people.

Morgan sighed. She had known this job was going to be difficult, but she hadn't realized that the first difficulty would be just getting into the same room as Leigh.

She trained with Max again and called Leigh once more after breakfast. Still no answer. Morgan grumbled under her breath as she read through the information Gray had sent her again. She sent

Leigh an email, on the off chance that Leigh was having phone problems, but somehow, she didn't think that was the issue.

The day passed slowly. Morgan tried to do other things, but she kept coming back to her phone, not wanting to miss a call from Leigh. Evening came and went, and still nothing from Leigh. Morgan was more than a little frustrated by now. Did Leigh want her help or not? This was just plain rude.

Finally, the next day at around lunchtime, she got a WhatsApp from Leigh.

Hi, Morgan. Sorry it took me so long to get back to you. Yes, I'm still interested in your services. Can we meet tonight? I've got an important charity function this evening that I don't want to miss, and Jake doesn't want us to go without proper protection.

So, it was the fiancé who had finally pushed her into action. Well, good for him. At least one of them was taking Leigh's safety seriously.

. . .

Sure, tonight sounds great. Where and when?

Leigh gave Morgan her address and they agreed to meet at five. The function was at seven, and Leigh apparently had to make sure that Morgan was appropriately dressed. As if Morgan couldn't dress herself. It sounded like a formal function, so she pulled out her best suit.

She hoped that Leigh didn't expect her to wear a dress, because if she did, she was going to be sorely disappointed. Dresses were alright until shit started going wrong and then it was a nightmare to try and fight or move fast wearing something totally impractical. Morgan had had this suit specially modified so that she had a greater range of movement in it than she had in an ordinary suit. If anything happened tonight, she would be ready for it.

She left early and sat outside Leigh's house in her car, not wanting to be too early and come at a time that didn't suit Leigh. If Leigh was willing to fire someone for folding a napkin wrong, Morgan couldn't take any chances.

One way or another, she would find a way to

convince Leigh to let her stay on, and she would solve the mystery of the death threats that kept coming in. Morgan knew that she was good at her job and she could catch whoever was behind this —if only Leigh would give her a chance to do it.

"This is a bad idea."

"Leigh, we've discussed this. It's the safest option."

"No, it's not, Jake!" Leigh hissed. "Don't you remember what almost happened with the last five?"

Jake sighed. "I remember, but keeping a secret isn't worth your life."

"Says you. You're not the one who stands to lose everything. If my mother finds out I'm gay, she'll disown me."

"My family will disinherit me too if they find out about me, as you well know."

"Yeah, but at least you have a savings account in your own name! Everything I have is in my trust fund, and my mother could have that taken away from me in an instant. I never studied after school; I have no skills with which to apply for a job, and no work experience. What would I do? Where would I go? Your savings account isn't enough to support both of us, at least not for long."

"I know. Believe me, I know. We'll just have to be more careful. I've already told Mike that we're going to have to sneak around even more when the new bodyguard arrives. And you've broken things off with Renee, so that won't be a problem."

Leigh knew that Jake wouldn't break up with Mike, even to keep their secret. The two of them had been in love for three years. She and Renee had only been together for a couple of weeks, and they were both in it for the sex more than anything else.

Ever since she had realized she was gay, Leigh had known love wasn't on the cards for her. She respected Jake's choice, but she didn't think she could ever give her heart to someone and then hide that from the world. Sex was one thing, but love was quite another.

"What if she gets too close, like the others? I know we said we'd do more to keep her in the dark, but part of her job is to investigate mysteries. What if the same thing happens with her?"

"Well, let's worry about that if it happens. You never know—maybe once we get to know her, we'll realize we can trust her with our secret."

"Not a chance," Leigh snapped. "I've told you already, there's too high of a chance that anyone we trust will go to the press or my mother, both of whom would offer them a high price for such scandalous information."

"Not everyone is motivated by money alone. Some people still have principles, you know."

"Well, I have yet to find them," Leigh muttered.

Jake nodded sympathetically. "They are few and far between, I'll admit."

He put an arm around Leigh, pulling her close into a side hug. Leigh sighed and relaxed into the embrace. She wasn't in love with Jake, but she loved him dearly. He was her best friend and had been ever since high school. They had bonded over their shared secret and had agreed to start "dating" when people began getting suspicious at their lack of love lives.

It was a perfect arrangement, really. She and Jake were free to pursue relationships or sex buddies as they chose, and Leigh got to live with her best friend.

Sure, there were times, late at night when she couldn't sleep, when she longed for more. She sometimes wished she could have what other people had—the simple joy of being able to fall in love and hold hands in public with the person her heart truly belonged to.

It wasn't for her, though. Leigh had long ago come to accept that, even though the truth did still hurt at times. She heard stories about homophobic family members coming around, but every time she brought the subject up, her mother started spewing hate that had Leigh fighting not to cringe. She eventually dropped the topic, as Amanda was just getting suspicious about Leigh's sudden interest in gay rights.

Amanda wasn't the type of person to fight for something that didn't benefit her personally. She gave to fashionable charitable causes, but more because of the status it gained her rather than actually caring about what she was giving money for.

"We can't go to that charity function without someone watching our backs. That threat you got the other day sounded more serious than any of the others, and the detective himself admitted that they haven't made any progress. Whoever's doing this is smart and covers their tracks well. We need the help."

Leigh knew that. It was why she'd agreed to bodyguard number six in the first place, but she was terrified that this would be one time too many, and her and Jake's secret would come out.

She'd just have to do her very best to push Morgan away. Leigh was naturally friendly and made new connections easily. She couldn't do that with Morgan. Getting too close to the last five bodyguards was what had gotten her into trouble in the first place. The closer they were, the closer they got to the secret, and that was unacceptable.

She was still debating whether or not to call Morgan and cancel when the doorbell rang. Crap, too late.

Leigh tried to smother her feeling of doom as she went to answer the bell.

She opened it and took in the woman standing in front of her. Did Morgan really have to be so attractive? It would be hard enough pushing her away as it was, let alone fighting off inappropriate thoughts about her. Even the way she was holding herself was sexy.

She was lean and athletic in a smart black pant suit, she looked like she could be a top level athlete in any number of sports. Her long brown hair was up in a ponytail, her tanned skin glowed and her green eyes shone with vitality.

Leigh realized she was staring and forced herself to stop, bringing her eyes firmly up to Morgan's (very pretty) face and she met those dazzling green eyes for the first time.

"Hi, you must be Morgan." She held out her hand and Morgan shook it firmly.

"That's right. It's nice to meet you, Leigh."

"Please, come inside. Can I offer you anything to drink?"

"Not right now, thank you. I have some questions about the threats you've been receiving."

Leigh did her best not to grimace. Questions always led to trouble, but she could hardly refuse to entertain them, could she?

"Of course. This way, please, Morgan."

She led Morgan to the lounge, where Jake was already seated on the sofa. Leigh curled up next to him. Jake put an arm around her, holding close. This much, at least, wasn't an act. They were both physical people and enjoyed close contact with each other.

Morgan got out a file of papers and a pen. "Is there anyone you know of who might have any reason to hurt you or Jake?"

"We've been wracking our brains about that since the threats started, but we're both coming up blank," Leigh admitted. "We don't have any enemies that either of us know of."

"Tell me more about your routine. What do you do on a daily basis? What are your habits, and when do you deviate from them?"

Here came the lying. Leigh squeezed Jake's hand, and he squeezed back.

So, they started to lie. Most of what they said was the truth, but they held back Jake's regular visits to Mike, as well as Leigh's trips to various bars to pick up beautiful women for the night. She hadn't been doing those recently, of course, but it was still dishonest to leave them out, given that they may well be relevant to the current situation.

"Are you sure that's everything?" Morgan prodded. "I need to get the full picture if I'm going to be able to help you."

"That's everything," Leigh said more sharply than she had intended to. "Now, if we're quite done here, I need to get ready for the function. And we need to get you ready, too."

Morgan glanced down at herself. "I'm ready to go."

"No, you're not. That outfit is entirely unsuitable."

Were it anyone else, Leigh wouldn't have cared what they wore, but she needed to antagonize Morgan at least a little bit. She didn't want Morgan thinking that she was nice or approachable, or they would end up with the same issue they'd had with the last five bodyguards.

"Well, what would you suggest I wear?" Morgan asked calmly.

"I've got some dresses upstairs that should fit you."

"I'm afraid that won't do. I need to be able to protect you, and if anything happens I can't do so effectively in a dress."

Leigh hadn't thought of that, but Morgan had a point. She supposed that Morgan's suit was actually fine for the charity function, but she made a show of huffing dramatically. If she played up the spoiled rich brat angle, maybe Morgan would lose any interest in finding out more about Leigh's life than she absolutely had to.

Morgan remained impassive in the face of

Leigh's brattiness. "I should check the house, just in case."

Leigh nodded. She was fairly sure that no one had gotten past the alarm system, but she supposed it was better to be safe than sorry. "Do you really think that someone is going to try to hurt me? I mean, they could just be trying to scare me."

"It's possible that their only aim is to scare you, but we can't assume that. We need to assume the worst to have the best possible chance of keeping you safe."

That made sense, though Leigh didn't like it one bit. "Check quickly, then. We need to get going."

Morgan did a fast but seemingly thorough search of the house before letting Leigh into her room alone to get changed.

Leigh and Jake sat in the back of the car together with Morgan in the front with the driver on the way to the event.

"What do you think triggered this? Was there anything in particular you were doing just before the threats started?"

Morgan thought of Renee, who had been a fairly recent development in her life. Of course, she couldn't tell Morgan about Renee. Besides, it wasn't like that was relevant. Renee was hardly the type to send death threats.

"Nothing."

Morgan frowned. "You know, I can tell when someone is holding something back. It's all about reading body language. A lifetime of studying martial arts has given me a pretty good idea of body language."

"Are you accusing me of lying?"

"Do I need to be?"

"How dare you!" Leigh held onto her fake outrage, because it was all that kept her from shriveling in embarrassment. She'd barely known Morgan an hour and already Morgan was on to her deception. This was going to be difficult. Maybe she had been right from the start. Perhaps she and Jake should just take their chances waiting for the police to come up with something.

Morgan turned her body and looked back at Leigh in the backseat. Leigh, again was struck by just how lovely Morgan's face was and how intense her green eyes were. "Calm down, Leigh. I realize that you don't know or trust me yet, but I'm only trying to help you. I can't do that if you're not entirely honest with me."

"I *am* being entirely honest with you," Leigh insisted through gritted teeth."

Morgan held her challenging gaze for a few moments before nodding. "Alright, Leigh. Alright."

Leigh got the distinct impression that Morgan didn't believe her and was only choosing not to pry for now.

She would have to worry about that another time. For now, Leigh did her best to focus on the charity event. She and Jake went arm in arm, throwing loving glances at each other and holding one another close.

Morgan walked a couple of paces behind them. She didn't exactly blend in, being the only woman in pants at the event, wearing minimal or no make up, and having a suspicious look on her beautiful face but she didn't seem self-conscious at all. Leigh allowed herself to forget Morgan's presence as she caught up with old acquaintances, ate and drank, and danced with Jake, as well as a variety of other men.

One or two women asked her to dance, too, but Leigh politely turned them down. If word of her dancing with a woman got back to her mother, she would be in trouble. Even if she tried to explain that she had just been being polite, it would lead to a huge fight. Anything that so much as hinted at gay was a cardinal sin in her mother's book.

Leigh found herself sneaking glances at Morgan throughout the evening. Her hair was shiny and neatly tied up off her face in a high ponytail and the look suited her. She carried herself in a way that was somehow graceful but also promised violence to anyone who might mess with her—and by extension, Leigh.

Leigh didn't like to admit it, but she felt safer with Morgan here, at least physically. Her secrets, however, were far from safe with Morgan so nearby and she needed to remember that.

Morgan followed Leigh to the bathroom and insisted on checking inside the stall before letting Leigh in.

Leigh couldn't help but indulge in a fantasy as she closed the door between herself and Morgan. If it was anyone else, she would have jumped their bones by now, but this wasn't just some random woman in a club who didn't know who she was. Morgan had all the information required to destroy Leigh, should she choose to do so.

Leigh caught herself wondering what it would have been like if she'd met Morgan during one of her clandestine trips to gay bars. They would certainly have had sex, should Morgan prove willing. Would they have taken it further? Would they have seen each other for longer than one night?

Of course, the situation now was all wrong for that kind of thing. Even if Morgan was willing, sleeping with her bodyguard would be a bad idea, not least because Morgan was being paid to be in Leigh's life. If she could be paid to guard Leigh, she could be paid to betray Leigh. She wasn't truly here for Leigh, like Leigh's sexual partners were. She was here for the money, and that meant Leigh couldn't trust her.

Still, Leigh couldn't resist being a bit naughty. She was still sitting on the toilet with her panties down around her ankles. she brought her hand to her clit, touching it lightly. Her own response took her by surprise. Her body surged and her mind provided filthy images of Morgan tying her up and having her wicked way with her.

Leigh felt her face going bright red, but she wasn't embarrassed enough to stop. She started rubbing herself until a soft whimper escaped her lips.

"Leigh? Are you alright?"

Leigh's hand flew away from her clit. "I'm fine."

She quickly pulled her lace panties up and

smoothed her dress down before opening the door. Morgan gave her a questioning look, but Leigh simply went to wash her hands. She hoped she wasn't as red in the face as she felt. Had Morgan figured out what she was doing? Even if she did, she surely couldn't know what thoughts Leigh had been having, right?

Leigh finished washing her hands and went back to the main room without looking at Morgan. She could hear Morgan's quiet footsteps following along behind her.

Morgan was clearly not happy with the answers Leigh had given her, because every moment Leigh wasn't dancing, Morgan cornered her to continue what was feeling increasingly like an interrogation.

Leigh was exhausted by the constant questions. It wouldn't be bad if she could just answer them honestly, but she had to dodge a lot of Morgan's queries, which was clearly leaving Morgan as frustrated as it was leaving Leigh.

Morgan kept pushing, though. Leigh didn't know whether to be annoyed or impressed. Morgan clearly cared about her job and didn't want to let anything get in the way of protecting Leigh—even Leigh herself. That, however, was small comfort when Leigh went to get a drink and found Morgan ready with another round of questions.

Leigh was relieved when the end of the event rolled around. At least at home, she could close her door and ask Morgan not to come in. She and Jake could pretend to be having sex—that had always worked well to keep their previous body-guards out for a bit. A few feigned noises of plea-sure and some banging on the headboard left them free to have a private conversation, as long as they spoke in whispers that someone standing right outside their door couldn't hear.

Morgan followed her and Jake into the car, but before she could start with her questions again, Leigh faked a huge yawn and laid her head on Jake's shoulder, promptly pretending to drift off.

She quickly felt bad about this tactic, because Morgan continued to interrogate Jake, and now he was left to face her questions alone, but she wasn't going to backtrack now.

When they got home, neither Jake nor Leigh needed to fake their exhaustion. Morgan checked their room before allowing them to retire for the night.

"I'll be up for a while yet. I want to check your

security cameras and patrol the outside of the property."

Leigh's insides squirmed guiltily. Morgan was doing her best to help them, and she and Jake were making her job very difficult, but what choice did they have?

"Thank you, Morgan. I will see you in the morning."

"Goodnight, Leigh, Jake."

Morgan left, giving Leigh and excellent view of her retreating ass. It was stunning. Blushing, Leigh forced herself to look away.

3

MORGAN

M organ wanted to tear her hair out. Trying to drag answers out of Leigh and Jake was like pulling teeth. She didn't understand why they would request a bodyguard only to be so wholly uncooperative when she tried to get the information she needed to protect them.

Sure, she could just follow Leigh around and then be ready if anything happened, but being fully prepared and understanding the nature of the threat was crucial to doing her job to the best of her abilities.

Did they not understand that she had to have the full picture if she was going to do her job properly? She had barely gotten any more information out of them than she had received from Gray. It was clear that they were holding back for some reason. The question was, why?

Morgan knew that she had to find out, no matter how resistant Leigh and Jake were to letting her in on the secret. She was going to protect them, despite their own best efforts to the contrary.

She checked the security cameras and, on seeing nothing concerning there, went to patrol the perimeter. She could see everything on the cameras—whoever had set them up had done a good job—but she wanted to familiarize herself with the property as much as possible. If she was going to be chasing suspects or sneaking Leigh and Jake to safety in the event of an attack, she needed to be completely at home with the house and the grounds.

Morgan lost herself in the familiar task of checking an area and getting herself acquainted with all the entry points and other relevant factors. The last thing she needed was to lose her temper with Leigh and Jake and end up getting fired. She needed to remain calm and professional, no matter how much she wanted to throw a fit and demand they tell her everything.

They obviously had some reason for keeping

secrets, and that reason was important enough to them to risk their lives over. Morgan feared that if she got herself fired, Leigh and Jake simply wouldn't hire anyone else, leaving their fate to the police, who had made it clear that they weren't making any progress on the investigation.

No, Morgan would have to stick it out and try to work with Leigh and Jake as best she could. She would never be able to live with herself if something happened to them simply because she couldn't keep her own frustration in check.

It didn't help that Leigh was distractingly beautiful with that long shimmering red hair and her soulful big brown eyes. Leigh's legs were long and her breasts were full and tempting. She was exactly Morgan's type—femme and lovely- except that she was engaged and probably straight. Morgan had never seen any evidence that Leigh swung both ways but reminded herself that this wasn't even an issue. Regardless of Leigh's sexuality, she was *engaged,* and Morgan needed to remember that.

The last thing she wanted to do was come between Leigh and Jake. The two of them clearly adored each other, and they made a wonderful couple.

After patrolling the perimeter, Morgan checked the locks on all the doors and windows before retiring to the guest room. She expected to lie awake for ages, mulling over the mystery surrounding Leigh and Jake, but it had been a trying evening and she soon found herself drifting off.

The next day, Morgan discovered, to her horror, that Leigh liked to go to the gym at five-thirty in the morning. Morgan herself liked to go early, but five-thirty was just cruel and unusual punishment.

"You don't even work!" she protested. "You can go at any time. And besides, it'll be crazy busy now, with everyone going before work."

"Most of my friends work, so we all go together at this time. Come on, Morgan, I want to get there as the doors are opening."

Morgan grumbled under her breath as she dragged herself into the shower, reviving slightly under the warm spray. She got dressed in her training clothes and followed Leigh to the car.

Leigh was in yellow lycra hot pants and a matching sports bra. She threw on a hoodie to travel, but Morgan couldn't get the thought of her body barely clothed out of her head.

And she was going to have to watch Leigh in the gym dressed like this for the next hour or so. She looked so different fresh faced, no make up, her hair tied up in a messy bun and Morgan liked this look.

Fuck.

Focus, Morgan.

"So, do you always go alone, or does Jake sometimes join you?"

Leigh shrugged. "We're nearly there. It's not far."

Morgan gritted her teeth. Seriously? What was wrong with that question? She didn't see how it could reveal anything secret, but Leigh clearly did.

"What kind of workout do you do?" Morgan tried.

This time, at least, Leigh seemed happy to answer. "I usually just run on the treadmill."

Great. Running—the most boring type of exercise. Morgan would need to run next to Leigh to be as close as possible should something happen.

"You don't want to do a class?" she tried. "Boxing is a lot of fun..."

"Nah, I love my running."

Of course, she did. Morgan resigned herself to

a boring time at gym, thinking wistfully of Max and her other regular training partners at her gym. She'd have to tell them all about this nightmare when she was back. They'd get a kick out of it, at least.

Leigh's friends turned out to be quite pleasant, actually, which was a nice surprise. Leigh had been so weird with Morgan that Morgan had been half-expecting her friends to be the same, but they were bubbly and friendly, and not nearly as closed-lipped as Leigh was.

Not that Leigh was closed-lipped with them. She chatted happily about her life as she ran steadily on the treadmill. She was learning more listening in on this conversation than she had in all of her questions to Leigh and Jake last night, Morgan thought sourly.

They ran for an hour before Leigh and her friends called it quits. It hadn't been as boring as Morgan had feared, mainly because she'd been so engrossed in trying to gather information on Leigh's life. She felt like a spy, but what choice did she have, when Leigh wouldn't answer her questions?

They returned to the mansion, and Morgan

would dearly have loved to go back to bed for an hour or so, but Leigh was already walking through to the dining room, where her private chef had breakfast ready.

Morgan sighed and followed her, doing her best not to stare at the way Leigh's hips swayed in those lycra hot pants when she walked. Her ass was round and inviting. It was entirely too sexy, and Morgan was only human. How was she supposed to survive living in close proximity to Leigh for any length of time?

She reminded herself that she'd been through much more challenging situations than unrelieved horniness. She would endure; she had no choice.

"I'll need access to your emails."

Leigh choked on her bite of toast, causing Morgan to hurry over and slap her on the back.

"What?" Leigh gasped after gulping down a few sips of fruit juice.

"I need access to your emails. I have to know everything about your life if I'm going to know it well enough to figure out who's threatening you."

"Absolutely not! My emails are private."

"Leigh, I'm not looking to exposé on your personal life. I just want to find out who's threatening you. You still want that, don't you?"

"Of course I do!"

"Then I need access to your emails."

Leigh bit her lip. "Let me think about it."

She spent several hours in her room alone thinking about it. During those hours, Jake came home. Morgan hadn't even realized that he'd left the house and berated herself for her lack of vigilance even though it wasn't Jake she was employed to protect.

"Hi, Jake. Where have you been?"

"Out," Jake said vaguely.

Morgan resisted the urge to roll her eyes. "I figured as much. Out where?"

"Oh, you know. Just around."

"I really need to know your and Leigh's routines if I'm going to get to the bottom of this," Morgan pressed.

"Of course, I understand."

He didn't say anything further or give any indication that he was going to share anything further. Morgan was getting ready to press some more when Leigh's door opened.

"Fine. You can have access to my emails. This is my username and password."

Morgan had a sneaking suspicion that Leigh had spent the past few hours thoroughly doctoring her emails and deleting the ones that she didn't want Morgan to see. This entirely defeated the purpose, but Morgan didn't suppose that explaining this to Leigh would make much difference.

"Thank you, Leigh. I'm sure it'll be very helpful." Not as helpful as it would have been if Leigh had allowed her to see the unfiltered emails, but maybe Morgan could still glean something from them.

Right now, though, she was more interested in Jake. Where had he been and why was he so reluctant to tell her? Granted, the reluctance wasn't anything new judging by what she had seen so far from both Leigh and Jake, but it seemed awfully suspicious for him just to vanish, possibly all night, and return without a word of explanation.

Leigh hadn't commented at all on his reappearance, which made Morgan suspect that this was a regular occurrence. Her first thought was that Jake might be having an affair, but if he was, surely he would make more of an effort to hide it from Leigh? No, it had to be something else.

What if Jake was leaving because he needed to compose his next threat to Leigh and arrange delivering it in a way that left no path to trace it back to him?

Morgan personally didn't see Jake ever threatening Leigh, judging from what she had seen of the two of them so far, but she had been wrong before, and she couldn't just ignore such suspicious behavior.

Leigh and Jake spent a couple of hours playing some complicated board game whose rules were beyond Morgan. When they finally separated, Jake going for a drink with some friends and Leigh going to the pool, Morgan followed Leigh.

"You should come swim with me, Morgan!"

Morgan did her best to keep her eyes on Leigh's face, because looking at Leigh's lithe body and full breasts in that red and gold bikini was doing things to her, and she couldn't afford to be distracted right now. Her skin was lightly tanned and her face covered in freckles as she smiled at Morgan.

Fuck, why is she so beautiful?

"It's best that I stay over here," Morgan explained from the deck. "If anyone breaks in now, I don't want to be in the water."

"Unless they're in the water too."

"I'll stop them from ever getting that close to you."

Leigh shrugged and did an underwater back-flip. Fuck, that made her ass look fantastic. Morgan felt herself blushing and averted her gaze, checking their surroundings for any sign of movement, but all was quiet.

After swimming for a while, Leigh spread her towel on the deck and came to lie in the sun. Morgan took her chance. "So, where was Jake last night?"

"Oh, you know. Out."

Morgan gritted her teeth. "I know that. Leigh, I really need some specifics from you. Where exactly do you and Jake mean by out?"

"I'm kind of tired. I think I'm going to have a nap. Chat later, Morgan."

"This isn't a *chat*, Leigh. This is important information that I need to have if I'm going to protect you effectively."

Too late. Leigh was already going back inside. Morgan followed her, debating whether to keep pushing or not. She decided to keep quiet for now. She was good at reading body language, and she could easily tell that Leigh was not happy with her.

She was tense and defensive whenever Morgan was around.

Somehow, despite the fact that Morgan was literally only here for her protection, she saw Morgan as a threat. Morgan didn't want to become the sixth fired bodyguard, and not just because she wanted to impress Gray and the other guards at the agency.

While Leigh had been acting strange with her from the word go, Morgan had gotten a chance to observe her, both at the charity event and at the gym with her friends. Leigh seemed like one of those people who you just couldn't find anything to dislike about. She was genuinely nice, funny and empathetic. Morgan would have been proud to consider her a friend, but it was becoming increasingly clear that that was never going to happen.

She would have to be content with saving Leigh's life—if Leigh allowed her to do so. Morgan was determined to do everything in her power to make sure nothing happened to Leigh, no matter what she had to do, even if that made her unpopular.

And what she had to do was going to make her extremely unpopular.

Morgan needed to start investigating Jake. She ideally needed into his emails, but if Leigh's reaction was any indication, he would delete anything important before allowing her access, if he gave her access at all.

No, she would need to be sneakier about this. She would start looking into Jake's past, as quietly as she could. Gray had some contacts in the government who could probably help her get some information on Jake's history. If he was hiding anything that gave indication that he might want to hurt Leigh, Morgan would find it.

She checked Leigh's room before letting her lie down for her "nap." Morgan was entirely certain that Leigh wasn't tired but calling her out on the lie wouldn't do any good. She got her laptop out of the guest room and took a chair to sit outside Leigh's room to wait out Leigh's escape.

While she was waiting, Morgan started to do some basic Google searches on Jake. Everything that came up on him was exactly as she'd expected. He was a good guy with no apparent skeletons in his closet. No one had anything bad to say about him.

Sighing, Morgan sent off an email to Gray, asking her to get as much information on Jake as she could. This whole thing could be a waste of time, but Morgan couldn't exactly not follow a potential lead.

While she waited for Gray to get back to her, she went over every interaction she'd seen between Leigh and Jake in her head.

What reason would Jake have to threaten Leigh? Leigh came from money and he didn't. Was it possible that their relationship was in trouble and he was sending the threats to scare Leigh, to make her draw automatically closer to him as a source of protection, all for her money?

It was possible, but Morgan just didn't see it. Jake's and Leigh's interactions had seemed genuine. She didn't think Jake was in it for the money.

Another reason, then? Perhaps Leigh was having an affair that Jake knew about, and he was threatening her to drive her back into his arms, maybe even hoping to make her suspicious of her secret lover.

That made slightly more sense. It would even explain why Leigh was so secretive. If she didn't know Jake knew about the affair, she would do anything to keep it from him—people who cheated always did.

Still, it didn't sit quite right with Morgan. Leigh didn't seem like the kind of person to cheat and it would soon be obvious with Morgan watching her if she was. Still, there was clearly something going on, something more than Morgan was seeing.

Whatever it was, she was going to make it her business to find out.

4

LEIGH

L eigh felt like she was going crazy, but she couldn't suppress the suspicion that Morgan was up to something. Of course, that was probably just her own misplaced guilt over deceiving Morgan.

And yet, it seemed that Morgan was behaving secretively, always closing her laptop when Leigh came into view, or hastily ending phone calls whenever Leigh approached. She had taken a step back with her barrage of questions, too.

This should have been a relief, but if anything, it made Leigh even more antsy than before. Morgan was still clearly committed to doing her job. She was up late every night going over security footage, and still insisted on checking each room before allowing Leigh into it.

She coordinated with event organizers to be certain that venues were secure before giving the okay for Leigh and Jake to go, and pushed through every morning with Leigh at gym, even though it was clear she hated running as much as she hated being up that early.

For someone who clearly didn't run regularly, it looked easy for Morgan. Leigh enjoyed seeing her in track pants, a sporty T and messy ponytail. Morgan was so athletic, she looked so at home in a gym. Leigh admired the lean muscles on her arms and hoped for the day Morgan would get in the pool with her so she could see some more of her long lean athletic body.

Why did she stop with her questions now? Leigh could only assume—perhaps with paranoia —that Morgan had decided to get her answers in another way. She certainly was spending a lot of her free time on her laptop and phone.

"Morgan?"

"Yeah?" Morgan looked up from her laptop, which was carefully positioned facing away from Leigh.

"What are you working on?"

"Just stuff to do with your case."

Leigh knew that tone—it was the same too-causal tone that she and Jake used when trying to avoid a question.

"Can I see?"

"It's best that I keep it private, I think. These investigations can get tricky if the subjects are involved."

So, Morgan was hiding something. Leigh folded her arms. "What is it that you don't want me to know?"

Morgan sighed. "I suppose we are overdue for a conversation. Not here, though." She glanced toward the lounge, where Jake was watching TV. "Let's go outside."

Leigh followed Morgan outside, wondering what she had to say that couldn't be said in front of Jake. Morgan was casual in jeans and a shirt and Leigh admired her ass in the denim. Morgan led her to one of the benches in the garden and sat her down. Her face was as lovely as ever in the sunlight and her green eyes were intense. "I think Jake might be the one threatening you."

"*What?*"

"I've been looking into him, and there are a lot of things that don't add up, Leigh. I know you don't want to hear this, but I don't think Jake has been entirely honest with you."

"What do you mean?"

"I don't know yet, but believe me, I will find out."

This was exactly what Leigh had been afraid of. Morgan was too good at her job. She had figured out their deception—or at least, figured out that there *was* a deception—and could even now be on the verge of solving the mystery.

"I think this was a mistake." The words fell out of Leigh's mouth in a tumble as she panicked. "I don't think we'll be requiring your services after all."

"Leigh, you know you do need me. Now stop panicking and tell me what's really going on."

"Didn't you hear me? You're fired!"

"What for?"

"For... For inappropriate use of my email account!"

"What does that even mean?"

Leigh had no idea what it meant. She was too busy trying not to freak out to come up with a proper lie. "Didn't you hear me? You're fired! Get out of here."

"No."

Leigh stared at Morgan. "What?"

"You heard me. No. I'm not deserting you, even if you fire me. Even if you stop paying me. I'm here to protect you, Leigh, I care about you, and I'm not going to stop until whoever wants to hurt you is behind bars. It may be Jake; it may be someone else. Whoever it is, I'm not letting them get near you." Morgan looked serious, but there was a kindness in her eyes.

Leigh felt her mouth pop open. It didn't make any sense. Morgan was only here because she was being paid to be here. That's the whole premise Leigh had been operating under. If that premise was false, how much else did she not know about Morgan? Was Leigh wrong about not being able to trust her?

She was unexpectedly touched by the gesture. "Fine. You can stay."

Morgan nodded. "As I said, I'm not going anywhere. Leigh, please reconsider your stance. I know there's something you and Jake aren't telling me. I have to know everything, or I have no hope of protecting you."

For the first time since meeting Morgan, Leigh was seriously tempted to do as she asked and tell her the whole truth. Maybe she could trust

Morgan. Morgan certainly seemed like a trust-worthy person. Surely, she wouldn't sell their secret, no matter how much money she was offered?

Leigh couldn't take the risk, though. No matter how tempted she was to trust Morgan, she had to be smart. The only true way to keep a secret was to ensure that no one else was privy to it; she had learned that the hard way by watching a dear friend being outed against her will by someone she had trusted.

"I can't," Leigh whispered. "Please understand, Morgan. I want to... I just can't."

Morgan sighed. "I hope that someday, I will earn your trust, Leigh."

"I hope that as well." Leigh realized that they had somehow gotten very close. Their faces were only inches apart. She didn't know who had leaned in, or if they both had, but now that they were in this position, she couldn't stop her eyes from flitting to Morgan's lips.

She wanted to kiss Morgan. Did Morgan want that too? She could swear that Morgan was looking at her lips as well. Leigh leaned in a little more.

Morgan suddenly pulled back, standing up. "I should check the garden perimeter."

"Yes." Leigh sounded breathless, even to her own ears. "Yes, that's probably wise."

Morgan walked away quickly, leaving Leigh staring after her in disappointment.

Reality came crashing back down on her. What was she doing? She'd sworn that she wasn't going to get close to Morgan like she had with the last five bodyguards, and here she was, on the verge of kissing her! Leigh needed to get her head straight.

Her head, however, didn't want to straighten, and presented her with persistent images of Morgan going down on her. Fuck.

"Morgan? I'm going to my room. I want to read for a bit."

"Sure thing. I'll be right there."

Leigh hurried her steps as Morgan caught up to her. She was worried about Morgan picking something up from her body language, but there was little she could do about that now.

Leigh closed the door between them with relief and went straight for her drawer. She grabbed her favorite vibrator and shoved her pants down around her ankles.

Her brain was still relentlessly serving up images of Morgan going down on her and Leigh was only human, after all. She reached a hand between her legs to find herself already wet. She spread some of that wetness up to her clit and turned on the toy, rubbing it lightly over the area.

Leigh moaned softly and quickened her pace. It was so good, but she wanted more. She stopped and hauled her very expensive, very effective dildo machine out of the cupboard. She slept with partners more often than she masturbated, but she masturbated often enough that she was glad to have this particular toy. She put some music on to drown out the sound.

It was already set to her favorite position, so Leigh only had to turn on and shuffled back toward it on her hands and knees. Before she did so, she grabbed another vibrator—a butterfly strap-on one that she fastened securely over her clit.

Then she slowly impaled herself on the thick dildo of the machine. She pressed the on button and it began thrusting.

Fuck, that was fantastic. It had been far too long since she'd used this thing. She adjusted the vibrator on her clit slightly, so that the vibrations were hitting her perfectly, leaving her gasping for breath.

Leigh started thrusting back, fucking herself

on the dildo at a pace to match its mechanical one. She thought of Morgan, wondering what it would be like to have Morgan fuck her with a strap-on. Was Morgan a top or a bottom? Surely, she was a top. It would fit her whole attitude. Leigh was happy topping or bottoming, but for Morgan, she only wanted her one way.

Leigh clamped her mouth shut, fully aware that Morgan was just on the other side of the door and would rush in if she thought that Leigh was in distress. If Morgan walked in on her like this, Leigh thought she might just die of embarrassment.

She pretended that instead of the dildo machine, it was Morgan behind her, whispering sweet, hot words to her.

Leigh closed her eyes and slipped fully into her fantasy.

"Don't you dare come yet, Leigh. You wait until I say so."

Leigh whimpered. "I can't. I'm so close, Morgan. Fuck. I'm going to come—I'm going to come now!"

"Don't you dare! Hold it in, Leigh. I know you can do it, sweet girl."

"I can't!" Leigh wailed. "Please, let me come, Morgan. I'm going to explode. I need it. I need it so badly."

"You need what I say you need, and right now, I say you need to wait."

Leigh's every nerve was on fire. She slowed down, so that she was merely rocking against Morgan's steady thrusts. She pulled the vibrator slightly away from her clit so that it was barely touching her.

It wasn't enough. Her orgasm couldn't be held off. The dildo split her in two as Morgan thrust into her without mercy.

"Put that thing back. I didn't tell you that you could take it off."

"I'm going to come," Leigh panted, even as she obeyed. "I'm going to come, I'm going to come, I'm going to come..."

"Not yet," Morgan warned.

"I can't help it—Morgan, please!"

"Just a little longer," Morgan whispered, running a soothing hand down Leigh's side, reaching for her breasts.

"That's...not...helping!" Leigh panted as Morgan started fiddling with her nipples.

"Come for me, Leigh."

Morgan twisted one nipple hard enough to send a spike of pain through Leigh's body.

It was the final piece that sent Leigh right over the edge. She screamed as she came harder than she ever had in her life, convulsing on the dildo, one hand over the vibrator on her clit, rubbing it in frantic circles as she took her pleasure. The pain in her nipple redoubled as Morgan gripped harder, sending renewed waves of pleasure through Leigh's body.

The orgasm drew on and on until she thought she might die from the sheer length and intensity. Surely, no one could survive this level of pleasure?

When it finally ended, Leigh fell forward, letting the dildo slip out of her pussy, catching herself awkwardly on one arm while she removed the vibrator from her oversensitive clit with the other.

"Leigh? Are you alright?"

Leigh was wrenched out of her fantasy by a sharp knock on the door. Morgan. Fuck, she must have been louder than she thought. "I'm fine, Morgan! I just... I stubbed my toe on the desk. I'm alright."

She stayed where she was for several moments, praying that Morgan wouldn't come in.

"Okay. Just checking."

Leigh breathed out a sigh of relief. She scrambled to put away her toys before Morgan found some other reason to come and check on her. She couldn't believe she'd just done that. She hadn't even realized she had a kink for orgasm denial, but Morgan seemed to bring out strange things in her.

Too bad she'd never get a chance to explore this with Morgan in person.

Leigh avoided leaving her room for as long as possible, but her stomach finally forced her out for lunch. She struggled to meet Morgan's eyes, sure that Morgan would somehow know her dirty fantasy just by looking at her.

Of course, that wasn't possible, but Leigh felt herself reddening every time she held Morgan's gaze for long. Morgan took it in her stride, like she had everything else Leigh had thrown at her. She truly was a devoted guard. When this was all over, Leigh would make sure to give her a large bonus, as well as hand over a glowing review to her boss.

Deciding that she couldn't be trapped in the house alone with Morgan right now—Jake and Mike were at the spa—Leigh texted a few friends until she found one who could meet her for drinks. Of course, Morgan tagged along, but it was easier to ignore her embarrassment over her naughty little fantasy when there were so many other people around them.

Leigh mostly ignored Morgan as she chatted with her friend, and Morgan made no move to insert herself into the conversation. She was considerate like that. She didn't interfere with any of Leigh's usual activities if she could help it.

Jake got back from his spa day practically glowing. He and Leigh faked having loud sex so that he could tell her all about it. Leigh even confessed her guilty fantasy about Morgan.

"So? Sleep with her. I've seen the way she looks at you. Trust me, she won't turn you down."

"You know why I can't."

"I think you're wrong about her. I think we can trust her."

"I think we can, too, Jake, but that's the operative word—*think*. Thinking isn't good enough. We need to *know* before we make a decision that could destroy both of us."

"I'll leave it to your judgment, but just know that if we're voting, I vote to tell Morgan. It'll help her do her job, and it'll make our lives a lot easier if we don't need to sneak around in our own home."

Leigh moaned loudly before jiggling the head-board a few times, banging it against the wall for Morgan's benefit.

"I know it sucks to have to hide at home—the one place we thought we'd never have to hide. I'm sorry, Jake. This is all because of threats against me. I wish you didn't have to deal with it too."

"Hey, none of that. We're a team. Now come on, let's finish up out little tryst and get to bed. You look like you could use some sleep."

They both "came" at nearly the same time. Jake and Leigh had both masturbated in front of each other so that they could describe to one another the noises the other made while coming. Leigh believed the results were both accurate and convincing.

When they emerged for dinner, Leigh still felt a little self-conscious around Morgan, but Jake put her at ease by being his usual self, distracting her with engrossing conversation, so much so that Leigh barely noticed that her plate was empty.

She said goodnight to Morgan and retreated to her room, reading for a bit before going to bed.

Leigh was a good sleeper and almost always slept through the night, which was why she was surprised when she woke up in the middle of the night, as suddenly as though someone had poured a bucket of ice water over her head.

She stayed where she was, some instinct warning her not to move or turn on the light. Leigh saw a shadow moving in the corner of her room, not a corner where the light from the streetlamps outside usually reached.

She froze, her heart suddenly beating double-time.

The shadow moved.

Leigh was certain now.

Someone was in her room.

The shadow lunged for her.

Leigh screamed.

5

MORGAN

Morgan was woken by the sound every bodyguard dreaded being woken by: her client screaming in terror.

She bolted out of bed and burst into Leigh and Jake's room, flicking the lights on.

What awaited her was a scene out of a nightmare.

Leigh was pressed up against the headboard, shrieking, her eyes on the looming figure that was fast approaching her.

Morgan couldn't make out anything about what the man looked like, as he was wearing a ski mask. All she could tell was that he was of average height and build. As if that would help anyone identify him.

She didn't have long to dwell on this, though, because he was advancing quickly on Leigh with a knife.

Morgan threw herself at him, tackling him to the floor. He immediately turned to face the new threat, trying to stab her through the ribs. Morgan rolled out of the way just in time and grabbed his wrist. He twisted it away, but she managed to get hold of his arm and she wasn't letting go for anything.

She wrapped her legs around his waist, focusing on holding him still while she disarmed him. She finally wrested the knife from his hand, but in the few moments when her focus was on the knife, he used the opportunity to escape her legs. Morgan hurried to put herself between him and Leigh, falling into a defensive crouch, the knife clutched in her hand.

The attacker appraised them for a brief moment before turning and leaping through the window. Morgan cursed under her breath as she followed him. it was dark outside and he was wearing black clothing, making him little more than a shadow. She dashed after him, leaping over benches and dodging around bushes.

It was over in a few short moments. He rounded a corner, and when Morgan rounded less than a couple of seconds later, he was gone.

"Fuck!" She stared hopelessly around, looking for any sign of movement, but she had lost him.

She ran back to the house to check on Leigh. She didn't want to stay out here looking for him in case he decided to double back for Leigh.

Leigh was still in her bedroom and jumped violently when Morgan climbed back through the window.

"It's okay. It's just me."

Jake had an arm around Leigh and smiled in relief when he saw Morgan. "We thought you might be hurt. Did you get him?"

"No, he got away," Morgan grouched. "Come with me. I want to check the security cameras, but I don't want to leave you two alone in case he makes another attempt."

The three of them went through to the surveillance room, where Morgan flicked through video feeds until she found the one she was looking for. She watched as Leigh's assailant vanished into the trees in the garden, then reappeared at a wall, climbed over it and went out of sight.

She sighed. "I'm going to call the police. They need to be informed, and they'll want to take some fingerprints off this knife. Are you both alright?"

"We're fine," Leigh said shakily. "I can't believe that actually happened. If you hadn't been there..."

Morgan wanted to take Leigh and hold her and promise her everything would be ok. Her big brown eyes were scared and she was pale beneath her freckles.

"Well, I was there, so try not to dwell on the worst-case scenarios."

Morgan glanced at Jake, frowning. Now that she thought about it, Jake hadn't been in the room when the attacker had struck. It was most suspicious.

"Where were you, Jake? You weren't with Leigh when the attack happened."

"I was asleep in my room, over there." Jake gestured to a door that looked to be concealed behind a tapestry. Morgan poked her head through to see another bedroom, with no door leading out to the corridor.

What reason would Leigh and Jason have to sleep in separate rooms, but go to such obvious attempts to hide it? She would have to ask them, but they both looked so shaken right now that she couldn't bring herself to do it. She'd save her questions for when they had calmed down a little.

Leigh and Jake sat silently in the background while Morgan was on the phone to the police. They seemed to be in shock, not that she could blame them.

Once she had reported everything and was sure officers were on their way, she made Leigh and Jake both some tea and convinced them to eat a few cookies each. Blood sugar was usually one of the first things to go in situations like these and she didn't need either of them collapsing.

The police arrived a few minutes later. Morgan described the attack. Leigh wasn't much help, becoming too distressed to give an accurate account when asked what happened. Morgan saw it all the time with clients. Jake tried to comfort her, but it was clear he didn't know how best to do so.

"Leigh. Hey, Leigh, look at me." Morgan took Leigh's hands in both of hers. "I am going to keep you safe. Okay? I'm not going to let him get you. You can breathe. You can rest. I promise, I'm going to be on full alert from now on. He made a mistake tonight. He's given us evidence to use against him. I know it may not feel like it, but what happened here puts us closer to catching him than we were before."

Leigh took a deep breath, bringing her eyes up to meet Morgan's. "Thank you. I'd probably be dead right now if not for you."

"Just doing my job."

It was a lie. Morgan wasn't just doing her job. She was emotionally involved and she knew it. It was dangerous getting too attached to a client. Such attachments could easily lead to bad judgment calls, but she couldn't help it. There was just something about Leigh. She wasn't like anyone Morgan had ever met before.

"Are we done here, officers?"

"Yes, I think we have everything we need. I'll leave an officer stationed outside for the next few nights, just in case."

"Thanks." That wouldn't be necessary, as Morgan wasn't letting anyone near Leigh again, but she didn't want to offend the police, so she kept that opinion to herself.

"You should get some sleep," Jake told Leigh gently.

Leigh shook her head. "I can't sleep. What if he comes back?"

"You're exhausted. You need to sleep," Morgan told her firmly. "How about we bring a blow-up mattress into your room for tonight? I'll sleep by the window. If anyone else wants to come in that way, they're going to have to come through me."

Leigh bit her lip. "I don't want to make you sleep on the floor..."

"It'll be fine. I've been camping before. Sleeping on the floor for one night isn't going to kill me."

"Thank you, Morgan. I'm sure we'll both feel safer with you in the room." Jake squeezed her arm. "I think I should also get some rest. We'll talk more tomorrow."

Leigh helped Morgan haul a blow-up mattress out of the camping supplies and pump it up. Morgan grabbed her bedding from the other room, but just as she was about to lie down, Leigh caught her arm.

"I don't feel right with you sleeping on the floor. Why don't... the bed is plenty big enough for both of us."

Morgan's mind immediately dove deep into a fantasy of holding Leigh close and kissing the back of her neck softly before turning her around and kissing her lips. She'd wrap her arms around Leigh and slip a leg between her as she—

"Morgan? Are you alright?"

"I'm fine." Morgan was glad that the light in the room was dim enough to hide how red her face was right now. "You really don't need to worry about it. I'm fine."

"I insist."

Morgan considered. She knew that sleeping in Leigh's bed was a bad idea, but she also knew that denying the request would raise more questions than she was willing to answer. There was no good reason for her to refuse, other than her completely unmanageable attraction to Leigh, and she wasn't about to confess that.

"Alright. Just for tonight, though. Tomorrow, we'll get someone in to put bars on that window and a lock on your door. No one is sneaking in here again."

"I'll feel like I'm in prison... but I suppose it's better to be safe and feel a little claustrophobic than unsafe and feeling fine," Leigh admitted. She pulled the covers aside.

Morgan took a deep breath and slipped into the bed, leaving as much space between herself and Leigh as possible. Leigh turned around so that they were facing each other, and in the low light, her lips looked so soft and delicious that it was all Morgan could do not to lean in and capture them in a kiss.

She's engaged, she's engaged, she's engaged, she chanted to herself. She simply couldn't kiss Leigh. It was not an acceptable option. "Goodnight, Leigh."

"Goodnight, Morgan."

Morgan turned away from the delicious temptation in front of her, so that her back was to Leigh. Leigh's breathing soon evened out in sleep, but Morgan lay awake, struggling to relax with Leigh so close next to her. She was beginning to wish she'd insisted on taking the floor after all.

Eventually, after over an hour, Morgan finally managed to drift off.

When she woke up, she and Leigh were thoroughly entangled.

Her leg was between Leigh's, and Leigh's arms were wrapped around Morgan's neck. Leigh's head was pillowed on her shoulder and Morgan's arms were around her waist.

Fuck.

How the hell did that happen? She harshly

berated her sleeping self for betraying her so, but there was nothing to be done about that now. She carefully tried to extract herself, but Leigh's arms tightened in her sleep and Leigh mumbled some protest under her breath.

Morgan desperately wanted to escape this compromising position before Leigh woke up, but she didn't see how she could do that with how tightly Leigh was clinging.

She tried once more to extract herself, but Leigh only stirred slightly and clung tighter. Morgan sighed. She supposed there was no avoiding it.

"Leigh. Leigh, wake up." She shook Leigh's shoulder gently.

Leigh's eyes fluttered open. She looked so beautiful like this, all soft and open, and Morgan was taken once more with the desire to kiss her.

Engaged, she reminded herself firmly.

"We should get up."

Leigh went bright red and immediately disentangled herself from Morgan. "I'm so sorry, Morgan. I don't know what came over me."

"It's not your fault. You can't help what you do in your sleep; neither can I, for that matter. You must have thought I was Jake."

Leigh nodded, still red in the face. Morgan was sure that she must look similar. "I'm going to shower." Leigh grabbed some fresh clothes and hurried into the bathroom.

Morgan went to stand guard outside the bedroom door. No way could her self-control handle seeing Leigh in nothing more than a towel when she came out of the shower. She was only human, after all.

Once Leigh was done in the shower, Morgan took her turn showering before joining Leigh and Jake for breakfast.

"I want to get someone in today to install bars on all the windows in the house, as well as locks on the bedroom doors. We are not having a repeat of last night."

Jake nodded. "Agreed. We need to keep Leigh safe."

"How long do you think this will all be necessary for? I mean, we can't live locked in our home with bars on our windows forever."

"It'll be necessary until we catch whoever is behind this. As to how long that will take, I'm afraid no one will be able to give you an exact answer on that one. I'm hoping the police can pull some fingerprints off that knife, but if the person isn't in the system, then that won't be of much help.

"You can still keep living your life, though. I'm not saying you can't leave the house; I'm just saying we need to be careful, more careful than before. I can't be awake all night every night, so at least if we know your home is fully secure that will help. I'll need to thoroughly vet each location we go to beforehand and ensure that it has an escape route should something go wrong. And I'm not leaving your side for anything until we have this maniac behind bars."

"I won't argue with you there. I don't even want to think about what would have happened to me if you weren't there last night." Leigh was earnest and lovely.

"I'm also going to modify my schedule. I'm not leaving you alone, either—not until you're safe."

"That's not necessary, Jake. That's why we hired Morgan."

"Two pairs of eyes are better than one," Jake insisted.

"He's right, Leigh. I'd appreciate his help. Unless you would prefer I requested an additional bodyguard from the company to help me? I'm sure that could be arranged."

Leigh paled and shook her head vehemently. "No, I don't want anyone else. Just you and Jake is fine."

Morgan wondered about this reaction, but she didn't suppose that Leigh was going to explain it to her any time soon.

"Do you have any plans for today? I think it's better to stay home for today, just in case your stalker is still hanging around."

Leigh shivered. "Yeah, I'm not leaving the house if you think he might still be nearby. I could use a massage. I think I'll call Melanie and ask her if she can come here."

"That's a good idea. I also need to make some calls. I've got a company I trust who can do the bars and the locks."

They spent the morning making calls and coordinating with the security company. Leigh paid a ridiculous amount of money to have them move her up in the line so that they could come and install everything today.

Once that was sorted, Melanie arrived for Leigh's massage. Morgan waited outside the room, forced to listen to Leigh's soft noises of pleasure, which somehow sounded more genuine than the noises she made when she and Jake were having sex.

She did her best not to let her imagination go into overdrive and failed miserably. By the time Leigh was done, Morgan was wet, horny and frustrated. She did her best to remain professional when all she wanted was ten minutes to herself in the bathroom.

She couldn't afford to take the time for such concerns, though. She'd never forgive herself if something happened to Leigh because Morgan couldn't keep her pants on.

She hoped that Leigh didn't have any more massages in the near future. Morgan wasn't sure if she could stand to hear one more soft moan from Leigh without escaping to the bathroom and rubbing herself frantically to orgasm.

Just the thought had her biting back a groan. Fuck, she desperately wanted to come, but that wasn't an option. Leigh looked relaxed and bright-eyed and was already talking about taking a swim.

Great, just what she needed—Leigh in a swimsuit.

Today was going to be torture.

6

LEIGH

Leigh couldn't help but notice the way Morgan looked at her more and more lately—like she wanted to devour her. It was flattering, to say the least. She wished that Morgan would make a move, but Morgan remained strictly professional, apart from her heated gaze.

She knew she shouldn't, but she was only human after all, and couldn't resist flaunting herself a little. She put on her skimpiest, sexiest swimsuit and swayed her hips tantalizingly as she slowly lowered herself into the water.

She glanced up at Morgan from under her eyelashes to see Morgan tense and a little red in the face. Leigh tried to remember that she didn't want Morgan to know her secret, but it was so difficult when Morgan was looking at her like that.

Jake joined them at the pool, shooting Leigh an amused grin when he caught on to her antics. They spent a relaxed afternoon by the pool, Leigh trying and failing to coax Morgan into the water.

The next few days settled into a pattern. Leigh and Jake would do various things around the house. Leigh bought some canvases and tried her hand at painting. It turned out that painting was not one of her talents, but it was a fun way to pass the time, as she was still nervous about leaving the house, even with Morgan.

Morgan was on her laptop most of the time, doing research into who might want to kill Leigh. She had finally convinced Jake to give her access to his emails, but of course, Jake had gone through his emails beforehand just like Leigh had and deleted anything that would tip Morgan off to their secret.

The police managed to pull fingerprints off the knife, but that didn't help much, as they didn't have any matching fingerprints on record. Morgan hadn't been able to give much of a description, either, thanks to the darkness and the ski mask.

It was all looking pretty hopeless. Leigh

glanced over at the garden through her barred window, feeling rather sorry for herself. Would she just be stuck behind bars forever, waiting for an attack that may or may not come?

At least she would have Morgan forever in that scenario, she supposed. As vehement as she had been in her resolution not to make friends with Morgan at first, that determination was quickly fading. She found that she loved talking to Morgan. The two of them got on really well and never seemed to tire of each other's company, which was a good thing seeing as Morgan's company was not optional right now.

"Leigh? I think I have something."

Leigh looked up from a truly dreadful attempt at painting a portrait of Morgan. "What is it?"

"There's an email in Jake's junk folder; I don't think he even realized it was there. Listen to this:

'Soon Leigh will no longer be a problem, and we can be together, my love.'

Leigh, are you sure Jake isn't having an affair?"

Leigh's heart seemed to stop in her chest.

This couldn't be happening.

She and Jake had only hired Morgan on the premise that she would be able to do her job without finding out their greatest secret.

That email definitely sounded like it was from an ex-lover, though, or at the very least, someone who had become obsessed with Jake. If Morgan was to have any hope of finding them, she had to know that it was a gay or bisexual man she was looking for rather than a woman. Not revealing that information would send her off in completely the wrong direction, and then what would be the point in even keeping her on?

"Leigh, are you alright? You've just gone white."

"I... I need to tell you something," Leigh whispered. Every instinct within her was screaming at her not to do this, but what choice did she have?

"Tell me, then."

Leigh squeezed her eyes shut. "I'm gay. Both Jake and I are gay. We're getting married to keep the ruse up for our families. We'd both be disowned if they ever found out and I would be left with nothing. No money. No home. I have no skills to get a job with. We're good friends, but we're not in love, and we see other people. That email sounds like it's someone interested in Jake. It's probably a guy; you should know that."

"Leigh, look at me."

Leigh reluctantly cracked her eyes open, fully expecting a reprimand for lying to Morgan for so long. Instead, she found nothing but tenderness in Morgan's green eyes. "Thank you for trusting me with this. I swear, I won't do anything that will result in your secret coming out. It's vital information that I need to do my job; you were right to tell me."

"You could get a lot of money selling this information to the right people," Leigh admitted. "That's why I didn't want to tell you before."

"I wouldn't do that to you. I care about you way more than I care about money." Morgan put her right hand on top of Leigh's and Leigh felt electricity pulse through her body.

"I know. That's why I told you. You're different, Morgan. I know you won't betray me." That didn't stop it from being terrifying to speak a secret she had been keeping since she was a teenager, but Leigh trusted Morgan.

"I would never betray you. You're safe with me, Leigh—in every way."

Leigh would later blame it on the heightened

emotion of the situation. She had spent weeks resisting Morgan, and in that moment, she was so overwhelmed with relief and gratitude that her resistance just crumbled.

She leaned in and kissed Morgan.

Morgan moaned into the kiss, knotting a hand in Leigh's hair and pulling her closer. Leigh thought she might die of happiness. The kiss was more intense than her wildest fantasies had promised.

They kissed for several frantic moments before Morgan pulled back. "You're sure Jake is okay with this?"

"Absolutely."

"And this is absolutely what you want?"

"More than anything."

That seemed to be all the answer Morgan needed, because she dove back into the kiss. Leigh had had her fair share of kisses, but kissing Morgan was like nothing she'd ever experienced before. It felt like she had been drowning before, and Morgan was oxygen. She never wanted it to stop.

The moment was broken by the shrill ringing of Leigh's phone.

"Ignore it," Leigh mumbled into the kiss, chasing Morgan's lips even as Morgan pulled away.

"It could be the police. You should answer."

Leigh sighed and picked up the phone. She felt like she had swallowed an ice block when she saw who it was calling.

"I've got to take this."

Morgan gave her a heated look. "We'll pick this up later, yeah?

The ice block in Leigh's stomach had no choice but to melt slightly at the heat in Morgan's gaze. "Definitely."

Leigh turned away from Morgan, trying to get herself into the right headspace for this conversation.

"Hi, Mom." Though she knew logically that Amanda couldn't tell what she had just been doing from her voice, she still had an irrational fear that she would suddenly be called out for kissing a woman.

"Leigh, hi. I wanted to check something with you. The seating arrangements for the wedding— who is this Mike, and how did he meet Jake?"

Shit.

7

MORGAN

"Mike and Jake met through Richard —he's a mutual friend. I believe they meet up for drinks once a week."

Leigh was doing her best to sound casual, but Morgan could easily see the tension in her body language. At least she now understood what was behind that. Leigh had to keep up the act in front of her mother. It must be a terrible thing to have to live in fear of your family finding out who you truly are.

When Morgan had come out, her family had been nothing but supportive. She knew she was lucky, but seeing Leigh's situation made her aware of just how lucky she was.

"No, Mom, I don't think they drink alone. If I remember correctly, they go out with a bunch of friends. I don't like to intrude on Jake's guy time with his friends, so I leave them to it. Yeah, that's right. Okay, I'll talk to you soon, Mom. Bye."

Leigh's tense shoulders relaxed as she hung up. "I think she's getting suspicious," Leigh admitted. "She's asking weird questions. Mike is Jake's boyfriend. I'm not sure what how they met has to do with the seating arrangements. I worry that she suspects Jake isn't as straight as she's been led to believe, and if she comes to the correct conclusion about him, it's only a matter of time before she does the same about me."

"It sounds like you fielded those questions as well as you were able to. It didn't sound suspicious to me, and that's with me knowing the truth."

"I hope so. I don't know what I'd do if she found out."

"Have you considered just telling her? Secrets have a tendency to come out, and it may be better to do so on your terms."

"I can't do that! She'd disown me. I'm not like you, Morgan. I don't have super cool skills that translate into a real job. I'd have nothing, and no way to support myself."

That was a tricky one, Morgan had to admit. "You have money now," she pointed out. "Why don't you use that money to study. Your grades at school were great—you certainly have the intelligence to take your education further. Then you would have employable skills, and you'd be able to come out."

"Even that would make her suspicious. I've never showed any interest in studying. Why the sudden change of heart? I wouldn't be able to offer her any truthful explanation, and she's already catching on to the fact that there's something going on she isn't privy to."

That was a good point. Morgan thought it would be worth the risk, but she was different than Leigh. She wasn't opposed to risk—that's why she was in the line of work she was in. Not everyone thrived in an environment of risk. Most people needed to know they were safe at all times if they were to live their best lives.

It sounded boring to Morgan, but she had seen it time and time again. What she called excitement, other people called trauma.

She wished she could do something to fix the situation for Leigh, but there was no fixing stupid. If Amanda was idiotic enough to refuse to accept her lovely daughter for who she really was, there was nothing Morgan could do about that.

The best she could do was help distract Leigh from her worries.

"How about I help you forget her for a little while, hm?" Morgan stepped into Leigh's space and took her hand. "Only if you want to, of course?"

"I think I'd like that," Leigh breathed. She was so beautiful. And so close. Her brown eyes were fixed on Morgan, her pupils dilated with lust.

Leigh was more beautiful than anyone Morgan could have imagined. The closer she got to her, the more beautiful she found her.

Morgan leant in and took Leigh's lips in a kiss.

She pressed her tongue into Leigh's mouth and Leigh opened to accept her, moaning at the feeling. They explored each other, their hands everywhere on each other's bodies as their tongues danced together.

Morgan's hands were drawn down to Leigh's breasts as though pulled by a magnetic force. How many times had she forced her eyes away when Leigh was in one of her skimpy swimsuits? Now, she didn't have to.

Leigh moaned as Morgan's fingers brushed

across her nipples. She was sensitive there, then. Good. Morgan pushed Leigh's shirt down so that her breasts were exposed. She wasn't wearing a bra. Morgan ducked down to pull one nipple into her mouth, sucking gently.

"Harder, Morgan," Leigh breathed. "Please."

Morgan smiled to herself and obliged her, sucking harder until she was sure it must be painful, but Leigh's positively filthy moan spurred her on. She let her teeth graze lightly over Leigh's nipple, drawing a loud gasp from her.

"Do that again," Leigh begged.

Morgan gently bit into the hard nub of Leigh's nipple.

"Fuck, fuck, fuck," Leigh chanted. She reached a hand between her legs and down her pants, but Morgan batted her hand away, replacing it with her own. She found Leigh soaking wet and swiped some of that wetness up to cover her clit before she started rubbing ever so slowly.

"Morgan," Leigh whined, "please, I need more."

"You'll get more when I say you get more."

She watched in satisfaction as Leigh's pupils dilated at her words. She kept up her agonizingly slow pace, ignoring loud demands her own body was making. She was enjoying making Leigh squirm too much to pay attention to anything else right now.

Morgan dipped her head back down to suck on Leigh's other nipple until it was as red and peaked as the first. Leigh's moans were becoming increasingly desperate, and Morgan finally took pity on her, giving her a firmer pressure as she increased the motions of her fingers on Leigh's clit.

Leigh was practically crying with relief as she bucked her hips up into Morgan's touch. Morgan removed her fingers, prompting a whine from Leigh, but she didn't give Leigh long to complain. She took hold of Leigh's pants and pulled them down over her hips and to the floor. She did the same with Leigh's soaking white lace panties.

Leigh was left with just her shirt on which was pulled down exposing her breasts and her hardened nipples.

Fuck, she is stunning.

Morgan pulled her shirt up over her head so she could see all of her.

She traced down Leigh's body with her hands eliciting moans and squirms. She knew exactly what Leigh wanted but she wanted to take her time and enjoy her body.

She loved the way Leigh's hips and breasts were wide and her waist dipped in like an hourglass- she was narrow just below her breasts.

She admired the red curls of pubic hair that lay at the apex of Leigh's thighs.

Morgan thought she might explode if she waited any longer. She dropped to her knees and parted Leigh's thighs and Leigh willingly opened for her.

Morgan's hungry mouth moved to Leigh's swollen wet vulva and her tongue tasted paradise for the first time.

Morgan licked her a few times, loving the way Leigh writhed on her tongue, before pulling away just enough to speak. "No coming until I say so."

"But Morgan—"

"You heard me. Don't you dare come until I give you permission."

She watched Leigh carefully but saw nothing other than naked arousal on her face. Morgan grinned in satisfaction and went back to licking Leigh, dipping her tongue into her pussy, tasting her before moving back up to her clit.

"Morgan, I'm going to come!"

Morgan pulled back but immediately replaced her tongue with her fingers, rubbing quickly and firmly, causing Leigh to squeal in dismay. "Fuck, Morgan, I'm so close! I can't stop it—Morgan!"

Morgan pulled her hand away just in time. Leigh moaned pitifully as her body tensed fruitlessly, but with no pressure on her clit, her orgasm eluded her. She tried to reach for her clit with her fingers, but once more, Morgan pushed her hands away.

"I told you, no coming until I say so."

"I need it, Morgan. Fuck, I'm going to explode if I don't."

"You need what I say you need, and I say you don't need to come yet."

Morgan was desperate to watch and feel Leigh's orgasm, but she was enjoying teasing and denying her too much.

She loved how Leigh whimpered for her touch. She loved how Leigh's hips moved as though begging her. She loved how Leigh's thighs involuntarily parted wider in invitation.

Leigh moaned again, her head tilted back, her hair tumbling down her back, her eyes closed, an expression of utter bliss on her face. Morgan loved that Leigh seemed to be enjoying this as much as she was.

She went back to touching Leigh's clit, slower

this time, mindful of how close to the edge Leigh was. Leigh was soon panting, her hands clenched in the cushion as she strained to hold herself back.

"Morgan!"

Morgan pulled away again, leaving Leigh moaning and writhing desperately beneath her. "Please... I need to come. I need it so bad. Morgan..."

"I'll tell you what. You get to make me come, and if I'm pleased enough with you, you'll get to come afterward. If not, you're not allowed to come until we do this again and I give you permission."

"Fuck, yes. Take your clothes off, then."

Morgan grinned as she stripped off and lay down on the sofa. Leigh's eyes were all over her body and she looked hungry to please. This was exactly what Morgan wanted. Leigh was desperate to please her.

Leigh moved to her knees on the floor and parted Morgan's thighs. She didn't hesitate in taking Morgan in her mouth and going to work with her tongue. It was readily apparent that Leigh was no stranger to going down on women. Her clever tongue flicked over Morgan's clit before dipping down into her pussy, pushing deep inside her, and then returning to her clit.

Morgan heard Leigh's own moans of pleasure and it was obvious, she enjoyed giving to Morgan just as much as she had enjoyed receiving.

Morgan lost herself in the sensations, feeling her thighs tighten as her orgasm drew ever closer.

"Just like that," she murmured. "A little higher. Oh yes, that's the spot. Fuck, Leigh, that's so good. Ah—Leigh, Leigh!"

Morgan gripped a handful of Leigh's hair and pulled Leigh's face tight between her legs. She came hard on Leigh's tongue, her whole body tensing and releasing as pleasure ripped through her.

Leigh kept licking her like it was the one thing she wanted most in the world until Morgan finally pushed her head away, panting.

Leigh crawled up so that she was level with Morgan. Her eyes were still blown wide with lust. "Please, Morgan. I need to come. Fuck, I need it so badly."

Morgan was more than ready to give Leigh what she had been thinking about for so long now.

"Lie back." Morgan kept her face impassive, not giving away any of her intentions. Leigh did so at once, allowing Morgan to start touching her clit again. Leigh was clearly still right on the edge of orgasm, because she was soon gasping and making desperate little whimpers that told Morgan she was tantalizingly close.

Morgan pulled back just as Leigh was about to come, drawing a despairing moan from her. "Please, Morgan. I was good for you, wasn't I?"

"You were so good," Morgan promised. "I just can't resist torturing you for a little longer. You're enjoying this, aren't you?"

"So much," Leigh breathed. "I need to come, though. I can't hold it, Morgan."

"You can," Morgan soothed. "Just for a little longer." She stroked Leigh's clit lightly, knowing that any careless movement could send her tumbling over the edge.

"I can't." Leigh was practically sobbing with need. "I can't, Morgan."

Morgan pulled back again, grinning wickedly. "If you can't control it, then I think we need to stop until you're feeling a little more in control."

"What? No! No, Morgan, please don't stop!"

"Let's take a break for a few minutes."

"No," Leigh moaned. She reached for her clit, but Morgan captured her wrists and pinned them above her head with one hand. "None of that. You're in time out until you calm down."

Leigh squirmed beneath her, squeezing her legs together. Morgan let her. She was only prolonging her own torture. Morgan waited patiently until Leigh's breathing had settled, though her pupils were still huge and her pussy was still leaking steadily onto the sofa. Just the way Morgan wanted it.

"Are you ready for more, Leigh?"

"More than ready."

Morgan decided to use her fingers on Leigh, wanting to be able to talk to her as she teased and brought her closer to the edge.

"Tell me what you're feeling."

"Feels so good," Leigh murmured, her breathing picking up again, despite how slowly and softly Morgan was rubbing. She was truly desperate now and ready to come at the slightest provocation. "It's like your fingers are reaching tendrils inside me, going so deep, all through my body. It almost hurts, it's so good."

"Do you have a vibrator in here, Leigh?"

"Yeah. Second drawer near the TV."

Morgan found a vibrating pink dildo from the drawer and turned it on. "No coming," she reminded Leigh.

She thrust the dildo into Leigh's soaked pussy.

"Fuck!" Leigh's legs tensed up and she reached automatically for her clit but stopped herself before Morgan had to stop her. She instead grabbed the cushion beneath her and began moving her hips frantically to meet Morgan's thrusts.

"Can you come without pressure on your clit?"

"I never have before, but I think now—fuck, Morgan, if you keep doing that...I can't—"

Morgan grinned and redoubled her pace. "You're so close," she cooed. "Just hold out a little longer, and I'll let you come."

"I can't. Please, Morgan."

In answer, Morgan turned the vibrator up a setting and started thrusting harder, fucking Leigh thoroughly. She brushed her finger lightly across Leigh's clit, the barest of touches, but even that practically made Leigh scream in pleasure.

"You can come, Leigh." As she spoke, Morgan put her fingers back on Leigh's clit, rubbing quickly and firmly.

Leigh started coming at once, crying out and arching up with the strength of her release. Morgan kept rubbing and thrusting as Leigh squirted and squirted, so much that Morgan wasn't sure if it would ever end. Leigh's orgasm dragged on and on, her whole body shaking with it.

When it finally ended, Morgan pulled the dildo out and turned it off. Leigh was lying limply on the sofa, a dazed smile on her face. She looked so incredibly beautiful.

"Worth it?" Morgan asked.

"So worth it," Leigh murmured. "Fuck, that was the best orgasm I've ever had. We have to do that again sometime. Sometime soon. Like, very soon."

"I'm glad you enjoyed it as much as I did." Morgan lay down next to Leigh and wrapped her arms around her from behind.

Morgan was struck by how right it felt to have Leigh in her arms like this. She had never been much of a cuddler, but she found that she never wanted to let Leigh go.

She knew it wasn't entirely professional to sleep with a client, but considering her boss was married to an ex-client, Morgan didn't think she'd get into too much trouble over it.

"Leigh, have you seen my—oh." Jake froze in the doorway and grinned at them. Morgan felt herself going red and wondered if there was any point in trying to pretend this was something other than what it looked like. Her quick assessment returned the result that it was entirely pointless. She and Leigh were quite obviously naked in each other's arms, their clothes in a pile on the floor and the sofa truly messed up from vigorous sex.

"Well, it's about time."

"Shut up, Jake," Leigh grumbled while Morgan snatched a blanket to cover them. Leigh didn't seem at all self-conscious, but Morgan didn't know Jake well enough to have him seeing her naked, even if he wasn't interested in what he saw.

"I take it you told her, then."

"Yeah. Actually, we should talk, Jake. Morgan, do you want to tell Jake about what you found?"

Leigh got up and sauntered over to her clothes, getting dressed at a leisurely pace. Morgan stayed where she was, her eyes flitting between Jake and Leigh. Both of them were completely at ease. Jake even seemed a little smug. Exactly how obvious had she and Leigh been about their mutual attraction?

Jake glanced at Morgan. "I'll wait outside. Shout once you're dressed."

"Thanks, Jake." Morgan waited for the door to close before dropping the blanket and going for her clothes.

"You don't need to be self-conscious in front of

Jake, you know. We usually don't hide anything here. He's seen plenty of my partners walk naked through the house to get breakfast. It doesn't bother him."

"It bothers me, at least for now. I guess I still need to get used to this situation."

"Yeah. At least Jake will be able to bring Mike over again, now. He's been complaining about how shitty Mike's apartment is. I offered to pay for a better one, but Mike is stubborn that way and he won't take the money."

"I hate to have to say this, but I'm going to have to investigate Mike. If this is about getting Jake away from you, that makes Mike a prime suspect."

Leigh rolled her eyes. "Mike's a sweetheart. He would never hurt me."

"Nevertheless, I can't just ignore a potential lead, can I? At the very least, Mike might be able to give me some valuable clues that could lead me to whoever is threatening you."

"If he had any idea as to that, he would have gone to the police already, I can guarantee that."

"Sometimes people don't know that what they know might be helpful. It could be a tiny tidbit of information that he thinks is completely innocuous but could crack the case wide open."

"You're much more than a bodyguard, you know. You're more like a bodyguard and a private detective rolled into one."

Morgan grinned. "That's one of the reasons I joined Gray's firm in the first place. I like her attitude. Her theory is that there's no point in guarding someone if you can't take active steps to end the threat against them, or you'd always at the back and just reacting rather than actually making them safe. She puts all new employees through a course with a couple of private detectives to give us the skills to find whoever wants to hurt our clients."

"It's a good theory. I'm sure it's held many of your clients in good stead."

"It has. That's why our reviews are so good." Morgan couldn't keep the note of pride out of her voice. She loved working for Gray and took pride her work.

"Well, you can talk to Mike, but don't count on him being able to give you anything useful. Jake, you can come in now," Leigh called as Morgan finished pulling on her clothes.

The door opened and Jake stepped back into the room. "What's this I hear about questioning Mike?"

"Listen to this, Jake. I found this in your junk mail. 'Soon Leigh will no longer be a problem, and we can be together, my love.' Does that sound like anyone you know?"

Jake paled and quickly sat down on the edge of the bed. "Absolutely not! I would never associate with anyone who would threaten Leigh."

"Sometimes, people can fool you. They may seem alright in public, but you only find out much later that in private is a different story."

"We know all about that," Leigh said sadly. "My mother doesn't generally go on her mad homophobic rants in public—she knows how unpopular that would make her—but when we're alone... it hurts to hear, sometimes."

Morgan squeezed Leigh's arm, wishing she could take her pain away. "Exactly. I need you to think, Jake. Go through everyone you've met in the last couple of months. Is there anyone who stands out at all? Someone who might have been acting odd around you? Maybe seemed a bit enamored with you—even obsessed?"

Jake was silent for a minute before slowly shaking his head. "I'm sorry. I wish I could give you useful information, but I just can't think of anything."

"I need to talk to Mike. Even if he isn't involved, he may be able to help the investigation. I'll also need access to the emails you two deleted before allowing me to see your email accounts."

Leigh and Jake exchanged a guilty look.

"I'm sorry, Morgan. I didn't mean to hold up your investigation..."

"It's alright, Leigh. I understand now why you did it. Just be completely honest with me in the future, alright?"

"I will be, I promise."

"With that in mind, I could really use access to your WhatsApps, too."

Leigh nodded. "Sure. I'll download WhatsApp onto your laptop and sync it to my phone."

Jake, on the other hand, bit his lip. "I'm not sure about that, Morgan. There are things that you'd... rather not see on my WhatsApp."

"What kinds of things?"

"Um... private things between Mike and me."

"I'm not interested in your sexting with Mike. Don't worry, I'll skip through it as much as I can. You don't need to worry about me being trauma-tized or anything. I may be a lesbian, but I'm not going to expire at the sight of a cock. It won't turn me on, but it's not going to bother me."

Jake finally nodded. "Alright. Just be prepared for some... kinky stuff."

Well, now he had Morgan curious. "I'll be prepared."

She glanced at Leigh. Would Leigh be interested in exploring that kind of thing with her? She'd love to have Leigh tied up and at her mercy, begging to come for hours before Morgan finally allowed her release.

Fuck, now she was getting wet. She forced herself to think of threats to Leigh's life, which effectively killed her arousal.

"It's late; I think I'm going to get some sleep. I'll have Mike come over tomorrow. You two should get some rest—or do whatever it is you're going to do tonight." Jake winked at them before going to his interleading room, closing the door behind himself.

Morgan turned to Leigh. "I'm not tired."

"Me neither. You up for another round?"

"Fuck, yes," Morgan breathed. She stripped so fast that she was fairly sure she must look like a blur to an outside observer. As soon as she and Leigh were fully naked, Morgan crawled over Leigh in bed, pulling the covers up over them.

Watching Mike and Jake was sweet. Morgan became convinced within the first three minutes of the meeting that Mike wasn't the one threatening Leigh. Leigh had been right—Mike didn't seem to have an aggressive bone in his body. He was soft-spoken with a quiet sense of humor that made Morgan think the two of them could be good friends, given time.

Unfortunately, Mike wasn't able to give her any more useful information than Jake or Leigh could. It left Morgan frustrated, but more determined than ever to find the person threatening Leigh and get them behind bars.

"I want you to make a list of everyone you've dated in the past five years. The likelihood of it being an ex is high."

"It'll be a short list. Mike and I have been together for the past seven years."

"And you've never... strayed?"

Thankfully, Jake didn't get offended by the question. "Never. We've been exclusive for all that time, and we're both happy with keeping things that way."

"That makes things trickier. Alright, we'll do it

this way. Make a list of everyone you've had prolonged contact with over the past year, as well as any incidental contact that stood out for you."

"I can do that. I'll get started on it right away."

"You and Mike should do the same thing, Leigh. I want to cover all my bases. Whoever this person is, he's interacted with at least one of you before, I'm sure of it. We just need to find that link and follow it straight to him."

It was a quiet day after that. Leigh, Jake and Mike spent the morning and afternoon poring over their calendars, trying to make an exact list of everyone they had come into contact with. Morgan checked in with the police, who still had no leads.

That wasn't entirely surprising, given that the police only knew half of the situation, but there was nothing to be done about that. Telling the police was out of the question, as it was sure to get back to Leigh's mother.

"What's next?" Leigh asked that evening, when the lists were finally complete.

"Now, the slog starts. I need to go through these and follow with every one of them. In cases like this, with so many potential suspects, I'd usually ask Gray to send a few others to help me, but given your situation, we can't risk introducing anyone new, not if we want to keep your and Jake's secret."

"Jake and I can help. Mike works during the day, but my and Jake's schedules are pretty open. We basically cancelled everything after that attack in favor of staying home."

"I'm not letting you out of my sight," Morgan said firmly. "Either of you. The threats may be against you, but it's clear that Jake is also involved, which means he's also in danger. I'm not sending you out to interview possible suspects."

"There have to be other ways we can help, though, right?" Jake asked hopefully. "Maybe make phone calls to check out alibis, or stuff like that?"

He had a fair point. A lot of the work Morgan had to do could be done from here. She didn't usually involve clients in her investigations, but she could usually outsource some help, which wasn't an option here.

"If you're sure. It'll be very dull work."

"I could use a dose of dull, after all the excitement recently." Leigh chuckled ruefully. "Bring on the dull."

"Alright. I'll do the first interviews tomorrow, and I'll bring back some stuff for you and Jake to check. If I'm lucky, I can get through four to five interviews in a day."

Jake grimaced. "There are at least four dozen names on those lists combined."

"I know. Like I said, it's a slog, but this is the job. We just have to keep plugging at it until one of our potential leads pans out. Don't worry, I'll make detectives out of you yet."

The next morning, Morgan anxiously checked all the cameras and locks on the doors. "You don't open any doors while I'm gone, you understand? Don't even go near the windows. Definitely no going into the garden. If the doorbell rings, ignore it. If there's anything that looks even vaguely out of place, you call me, understand?"

"We understand, Morgan. Don't worry, I'm not going to put Leigh's life in any more danger than it already is. We'll err on the side of caution."

"Are you sure you don't want me to have Gray send someone over to protect you while I'm gone?"

"We're sure," Leigh said at once. "You know now why we were so reluctant to take on new bodyguards in the first place. Someone Gray sends would be particularly dangerous, what with the investigation skills you're all trained in. Don't worry, we'll be fine for a couple of hours."

Morgan could only hope that was true. She'd never forgive herself if something happened to Leigh while she wasn't there to protect her. She couldn't think of a way around this, though and the house was very secure now at least. She had to do the interviews if she was to have a hope of catching the person after Leigh, and such interviews couldn't be done over the phone.

Morgan needed to be able to judge whether the person she was talking to was telling the truth or not and seeing their body language was essential for that. She checked the locks on the doors once more before reluctantly going to her car. She made sure her phone was on loud so she would be sure not to miss a call from Leigh.

She was already anxious and on edge, and she hadn't even left yet. She'd better get her head together if she was going to do her job properly. She had to present a calm front when interviewing suspects, even if internally she was far from calm and worrying about Leigh's safety.

One thing was for sure, today promised to be a long day.

8

LEIGH

L eigh knew she was in trouble, and not just because Morgan and the police were no closer to finding her stalker.

No, she was in trouble because she was falling for Morgan in a way she'd never fallen for anyone before. Every time they were together, Leigh was consumed with bliss that threatened to overturn the way she lived her life.

She started having crazy, dangerous thoughts —thoughts like doing as Morgan suggested and studying so that she could get a job and support herself in order to come out to her mother. She wanted to be able to walk through a mall holding Morgan's hand. She wanted to be able to kiss her without worrying about who was watching.

Morgan had been more than understanding about Leigh's need for secrecy, but Leigh was all too aware that she was forcing Morgan into a life she'd never asked for.

Morgan had been out for as long as she knew she was gay, since her early twenties. She'd never hidden before and had never had the desire to do so. She insisted that Leigh was worth it, but Leigh still felt bad every time they had to act like they were nothing more than acquaintances in public.

She wanted to be able to show the world how proud she was to have Morgan as her girlfriend.

For that matter, she wanted to be able to call Morgan her girlfriend. They still hadn't discussed exactly what they were. For now, they were both focusing on the threat facing Leigh, but sooner or later, they would need to have that conversation.

What would happen after Morgan caught whoever was after Leigh? Leigh had complete faith that Morgan would do so, sooner or later. After that, she'd be on to her next job. Would she and Leigh stay together, or was what they had more a thing of convenience, a brief moment of pleasure while circumstances had them living in the same home?

Leigh knew she should just bite the bullet and

start the conversation, but she was afraid—afraid that Morgan didn't feel the same way. What if Morgan gently told her that she had never thought of what they had as anything more than extremely hot sex? Leigh didn't know how her heart would survive it.

Of course, delaying wasn't going to help anything, but Leigh wanted to hold onto this beautiful, fragile moment in time while they still had it.

"Leigh? Earth to Leigh? Are you alright?"

She blinked to find Jake waving is hand in front of her face. "Sorry, Jake, what were you saying?"

"Nothing important. I'm more interested in what has you so zoned out."

Leigh sighed. "It's Morgan," she admitted.

"Are things not going well between the two of you?"

Leigh glanced down the corridor to check that Morgan was still in the shower before turning back to Jake. "Things are going very well; that's just it. I really like her, Jake. Like, a lot."

"And you're scared."

Leigh nodded miserably.

"I felt the same with Mike at first. It's a good thing, Leigh. Being scared means you're invested."

"Being invested means I'm liable to get my heart broken."

"Or it means you could get your heart made whole in a way only your soulmate can do. Morgan could be the one for you."

"I think she might be," Leigh admitted. "I just don't know if she feels the same."

"Talk to her. That's the only way you're going to figure this out."

"I can't, at least not yet. I need to be able to look her in the eye when I ask her to be mine, and to do that... I think I need to come out."

Jake stiffened. "You know why that's not an option."

"It's not an option now, but Morgan had an idea. I have money, at least until Amanda disowns me. I could use that money to study, to get some good skills under my belt. That way, when I do come out and she disowns me, I can get a job and support myself."

"What about me?" Jake's usually easy-going tone had suddenly turned icy. "Did you think of that, Leigh? If you come out, my family is sure to figure out our ruse. They'll never speak to me again."

"That's easy enough to solve. I'll pay for you to

study, too. We'll both get jobs at the end of this. Working will take some adjustment, but it'll be worth it if we can be who we are to the world."

"That's not your decision to make, not for me! It's not just about the money, Leigh. I don't want to be exiled from my family. I'll never be able to see my nieces and nephews again. I'll be completely alone in the world. I'll be as good as dead to them. I don't want that."

"If they can't accept you for who you are, then they don't deserve to have you in their lives."

"Again, that's not your choice to make. They're my family, and I get to decide whether or not I want them in my life. Sure, they may not be perfect, but they're still the people who raised me and I still love them. I know you're not close with your mom, but you know how close I am with my family. I can't believe you'd ask me to give that up. It's not your choice to make."

"I don't get to make the choice for you as to whether or not you come out, but whether I come out *is* my choice, Jake!"

"And your choice affects me! We're supposed to be in this together, Leigh! We agreed from the start that we're in this for life. Coming out isn't in the cards for either of us, ever."

"Yeah, well maybe I've changed my mind."

"You're being selfish," Jake accused.

"You're being controlling," Leigh shot back.

The two of them glared at each other for several long moments before Jake turned and stormed out of the room.

Leigh's heart squeezed as she watched him go. She and Jake had never had a real fight before. She didn't have much time to process before the bathroom door opened and Morgan came through.

"Leigh, do you—hey, what's wrong?"

"Jake and I had a fight," Leigh admitted.

"Oh honey, I'm sorry. What happened?"

Morgan perched on the edge of the bed and listened as Leigh described the fight.

"Give him time," she said when Leigh was done. "It's a big mental adjustment for him. He's gone years thinking that the two of you are going to stay in the closet forever. He's not thinking rationally right now."

"What if he's right? Maybe it would be a selfish decision. Jake and I had an agreement, after all."

"An agreement that may not always work for you. You get to make the right decisions for you, Leigh. If you feel like you want to come out, then no one has the right to stop you."

Leigh nodded miserably. "I just hate being at odds with Jake."

"Would you like to talk about it more, or do you want me to make you forget about the fight?"

"Forget, please," Leigh said at once. She didn't want to think about the fight any more than strictly necessary.

"Then I have a surprise for you. Hang on, I'll go get it."

Morgan came back with... was that satin rope?

"Is that for what I think it's for?"

"Only if you want to."

"I want to." Leigh had fantasized about being tied up by Morgan more than once, fantasies that never failed to get her off.

"Then take your clothes off."

Morgan stripped at the same time as Leigh, tossing her clothes in a pile on the floor. Leigh lay back on the bed, already breathless with anticipation. Morgan tied first one wrist then the other to opposite sides of the headboard. What Leigh didn't expect was for Morgan to loop the long rope around to her ankles, tying them to the bedposts so that her legs were spread wide apart. She felt wide open and vulnerable.

"Tell me if you want the ropes removed at any time."

"I will, Morgan." Leigh tugged on the ropes, satisfied with how little give they had.

"Now, I'll have my wicked way with you."

"Yes, please."

"As per usual, no coming until I say so."

"Yes, Morgan."

Leigh was getting good at this now. After many accidental orgasms, she was finally learning some control.

On the other hand, as Morgan got to know her better, she was learning exactly how to touch Leigh to drive her wild and make her lose all control. It became a game between them, a game neither of them ever seemed to tire of.

Morgan started at Leigh's breasts, nibbling softly on her nipples.

"Please, harder. That feels so good, Morgan."

Morgan rewarded her with a sharp bite on one nipple, sending a spike of arousal through Leigh's body. Before Morgan, she hadn't known that she liked her nipples being bitten, but now that she knew, there was no going back. The harder Morgan's teeth sank into her, the more Leigh's clit throbbed and the wetter her pussy got.

Morgan knew very well the effect this had on Leigh and spent time worrying at Leigh's nipples with her teeth, driving Leigh crazy with desire. Leigh tried to reach down to touch her clit, to offer herself some relief, but of course, her hands were tied, which sent another flush of arousal through her body.

"Morgan, I need you. I need you so bad."

"Oh, I know, my impatient girl. You're so good for me."

Morgan moved down, laying her tongue over Leigh's clit. Leigh jerked up into the feeling, but Morgan simple withdrew, waiting for Leigh to settle. Leigh pouted but let her hips come back to the bed.

Morgan started once more, licking softly and lightly. It was enough to drive Leigh crazy but too light to give her any real relief. As she was licking, Morgan reached up and grabbed one of Leigh's nipples, squeezing it between her fingers and twisting.

It felt almost like a bite, different in the most tantalizing way. Leigh moaned and struggled against the ropes, but they didn't give. Morgan suddenly changed tack, licking Leigh more firmly, and now Leigh was panting through gritted teeth, trying with all her might not to come.

Morgan slipped a finger inside Leigh's pussy, moving it around until she found Leigh's G-spot. She battered the spot relentlessly while licking Leigh's clit and twisting her nipple progressively harder and harder.

Leigh couldn't withstand this triple assault. "Morgan, I'm going to come! Right fucking now, Morgan!"

Morgan pulled back with her mouth but kept working Leigh's pussy and nipple with her fingers. "We've barely even started. You need to do better than that, Leigh."

Leigh moaned as a fresh wave of desire went through her body. She pulled fruitlessly at the ropes. Something about being tied up had her body tingling in all the best ways. Somehow, she didn't think that all the self-control she had learned over the past few weeks was going to be worth shit right now.

Morgan started licking her again, firm and long and deep.

"Morgan, I can't, I—fuck!"

Leigh came, and came hard. Morgan pulled away the moment she realized what was happening, but Leigh's body was way ahead of her. She screamed as her orgasm continued untouched, pulling so hard on the ropes it was painful, and that pain adding the most delicious edge to the orgasm.

Morgan watched in bemusement as Leigh came down, panting hard and looking at her with wide eyes.

"Oops," Leigh whispered.

"Oops indeed. I guess that means you like being tied up?"

"So much, Morgan. Please, let me make you come?"

Morgan nodded. "I'm going to sit on your face. You're going to make me come like a good girl, and after that, you're not coming for two weeks."

"What! Two weeks?"

"That's right. Every night of those two weeks, I'm going to tie you up and lick you until you scream. If you come again without permission, I'm adding another two weeks."

Leigh moaned in dismay but couldn't deny the hot bolt of arousal Morgan's words sent through her. She loved the idea of being driven to her limits and tortured for an entire two weeks. She couldn't even imagine how intense the orgasm would be after that amount of time.

Morgan didn't even untie her before coming to sit on Leigh's face.

"If you need me to stop or pause, snap your fingers. Show me now that you can do it."

Leigh snapped twice, which seemed to satisfy Morgan, because she lowered herself onto Leigh's eager tongue a moment later.

Leigh knew Morgan's body now as well as Morgan knew hers, and she was familiar with exactly how to get Morgan off in the way she liked. Morgan liked it hot and fast. She rolled her hips, pressing herself down onto Leigh's tongue mercilessly.

Leigh loved it when Morgan used her like this, like she was nothing more than Morgan's sex toy. It made her feel beautiful and desired and loved.

Morgan was soon crying out on her tongue, her hands clenched on the headboard. Leigh knew when she was close by the way her hips stuttered and redouble her efforts. Morgan tensed and cried out as her pussy gushed all over Leigh's face.

Leigh kept licking as best she could until Morgan moved off her.

"Good girl." She kissed Leigh and licked her

own arousal from Leigh's face and then started untying the ropes. "Now, you're not to touch yourself at all. I'm the only one who gets to touch you during these two weeks, and when I do, absolutely no coming, do you understand?"

"Yes, Morgan."

Morgan grinned. "You still good?"

"Beyond good. This is going to be so much fun."

"I'm glad you think so too. I'm not kidding about adding two weeks for every illegal orgasm, though. And if you have more than two, I'm not going to touch you at all until I've decided you've gained enough self-control."

Fuck, that was terrifying, but so arousing at the same time.

This was going to be a long two weeks.

Leigh was practically vibrating out of her skin with need. Four weeks since she had last come, thanks to the extra two Morgan added when she came by accident just the day before her original two weeks was up.

Every day for those four weeks, sometimes two

or three times a day, Morgan had subjected her to the most delicious torture imaginable. Some days, Leigh literally sobbed as she begged to come, but Morgan remained firm. Leigh would come before four weeks only if she decided to end the game they were playing.

Leigh was enjoying the game far too much to end it.

But the time had finally arrived. This was the day. She just had to survive Morgan teasing and testing her for a little bit longer, and then she would *finally* be allowed to come.

She and Morgan were already naked in bed. Morgan trailed a hand between Leigh's legs, humming softly at what she found.

"You're already wet."

"I'm wet practically all the time nowadays," Leigh grumbled. "All I can think about is sex. I'm supposed to be planning a wedding, and I can barely concentrate over the sound of my brain screaming for an orgasm from my secret lover."

Morgan pulled back, giving Leigh a serious look. "If this is interfering with your life too much, we can—"

"No! I swear, I'm okay. I'm loving this, Morgan."

"Good. I'm not going to tie you up. I don't think we'll test your self-control that way just yet."

Nothing brought Leigh closer to the edge than being tied.

"I'm going to lick you for a bit. If you can hold out until I say so, you get to come. If not... six weeks."

Leigh wouldn't survive six weeks. She would be the first person in history ever to die of horniness.

Morgan didn't give her time to mentally prepare. She spread Leigh's folds with one swift movement and gave her a long, slow lick.

Leigh cried out, writhing on Morgan's tongue. Everything was so intense, and she was already so close. She'd been so close for days now, afraid even to wash herself properly in the shower lest she accidentally come from the contact.

Morgan licked and licked until Leigh thought she might lose her mind. They must be getting close now. Surely, Morgan would let her come soon. She couldn't hold on much—

The doorbell rang.

Fuck.

Fuck, fuck, fuck, she'd completely forgotten. In her wild state of need, Leigh had let her mother's visit slip her mind.

"Leigh? What's wrong?"

Leigh was already scrambling to get dressed. "It's my mom. She's here to talk about the wedding. Fuck, I'm so sorry, Morgan, I forgot."

Morgan leaped out of bed and started getting dressed too, laughing at the situation, but she paused to give Leigh a heated look. "We'll finish this later."

Leigh moaned. She was soaking wet and her clit throbbed and ached.

She didn't know how she was going to survive until later.

9

MORGAN

Morgan had never been so frustrated and so turned on at the same time. Watching Leigh writhe under her touch, so desperate for release, did things to her. Leigh may be ready to come out of her skin with need, but the truth was that Morgan wasn't far behind her.

Sure, she'd been having regular orgasms, unlike Leigh, but it felt like the more Leigh made her come, the more she needed it. She could think of little else but getting this meeting over with as quickly as possible and getting Leigh back into bed.

Morgan decided that she would make Leigh

get her off before allowing her to come. She couldn't wait much longer.

"Leigh."

Morgan realized that she had followed Leigh downstairs, too lost in a haze of lust to really notice what was going on around her. Amanda and Leigh exchanged what looked like a very awkward hug. Morgan took up her position at the door of the room, forcing herself to look around for threats. She was Leigh's bodyguard after all, not her girlfriend and she needed to remember that.

Over the past four weeks, Leigh had received two more threatening letters, but there had been no more attempts on her life. Morgan suspected that she had scared the stalker off, at least for now. She was still investigating the many leads that Leigh, Jake and Mike had given her, but it was slow going.

Morgan tried to pay attention to Leigh and Amanda's conversation. It was something about place settings at the wedding. She saw Leigh shifting uncomfortably in her seat and had to suppress a smile. She knew how uncomfortably wet Leigh must be. She couldn't wait for this to be over. She was going to take Leigh to bed and begin truly taking her apart.

Morgan seriously considered excusing herself to the bathroom to rub one out to the thought of what she was going to do to Leigh but decided that it would be even more delicious to wait. She was just immersing herself in a fantasy of the sounds Leigh would make when she was finally allowed to come when the window exploded inward.

All sexy fantasies vanished from Morgan's mind at once as a wave of cold fear overtook her. She lunged across the room, praying that she could somehow move faster than a bullet.

She couldn't move faster than a bullet.

Morgan barreled into Leigh just as the bullet hit. The two of them went tumbling to the floor in a splatter of blood.

Morgan was up and running at once. As much as her heart demanded that she stay and check if Leigh was even still alive, she knew that if she didn't stop Leigh's attacker, another shot could be coming at any moment.

She leaped through the broken window, but it was too late—there was no one in sight. Morgan swore as she looked around, but there was no sign of where he could have gone; he could have run off in any direction. Morgan had sacrificed her chance to catch him when she had chosen to go for Leigh.

She cursed again as she scrambled back through the window, heedless of the broken glass scraping at her.

She almost collapsed in relief when she saw Leigh sitting up, covered in blood and shaken, but *alive.*

Amanda was on the phone to the paramedics, which left Morgan free to hurry over to Leigh. It looked like she had pushed Leigh out of the way just enough to turn what would have been a chest shot into a shoulder shot.

Morgan had never been so grateful for anything in her life.

She had also never hated herself as much as she did in this moment.

This was all her fault. She'd been so immersed in her stupid, unprofessional thoughts about fucking her client that she had completely lost sight of what her actual job here was.

Leigh could have been killed because of her. As it was, Leigh was injured, and it was all Morgan's fault. She had no idea how bad it was. Leigh could lose use of her arm, for all Morgan knew.

"Is he gone?" Leigh was trembling, tears running down her beautiful face. Morgan didn't deserve to wallow in guilt while Leigh needed her.

She lifted a hand to stroke Leigh's face, only to drop it when she realized that Amanda was watching them.

"He's gone. You're safe now, Leigh."

Amanda rounded on Morgan. "What do you think you're doing, letting someone get that close to her! I thought you were supposed to be protecting her?"

Morgan couldn't think of a single word to defend herself.

"Give it a rest, Mom. Morgan pushed me out of the way just in time—or would you have preferred me to be hit in the chest."

"I suppose not," Amanda grumbled, but she was still eyeing Morgan unhappily.

Sirens were sounding in the distance. Morgan carefully put pressure on Leigh's shoulder, hating herself as Leigh gasped in pain.

"I'm sorry, but I have to slow the bleeding while we wait for the paramedics to get here. It doesn't look too bad, but you're still losing some blood."

"Just do it," Leigh said with gritted teeth. She closed her eyes as Morgan re-applied pressure. Amanda went outside to let the paramedics in, giving Leigh and Morgan a precious moment alone. Morgan pressed a kiss to Leigh's forehead.

"I'm so sorry, Leigh. I should have stopped this from happening."

"Don't be ridiculous; you saved my life. This is not your fault."

Morgan knew it was, but they had no chance to discuss it further, because Amanda and the paramedics were coming into the room.

Amanda insisted on being the one to ride with Leigh in the ambulance, and neither Leigh nor Morgan protested. Jake was out on a date with Mike, and it would look very suspicious if Leigh chose anyone other than him to take Amanda's place beside her on her way to the hospital.

Morgan got into her car and followed the ambulance as quickly as she dared. By the time she arrived at the hospital, Leigh had already been taken into surgery to remove the bullet. She skulked in the background, eavesdropping on the conversation between Amanda and Leigh's doctor.

It seemed that Leigh should make a full recovery. She'd have some rehab to do to get her arm working optimally again, but as long as she kept that up, she should be good.

This did little to ease Morgan's guilt. Leigh would be in a sling for days and sore for weeks. She'd have months of rehab before she was completely right. Morgan should have been the one who got shot. She should be the one in surgery and in pain, not Leigh.

The realization dawned on her like stepping into a nightmare.

There was only one thing to do.

She had to break things off with Leigh.

The thought nearly brought Morgan off her feet. She staggered to the nearest chair. Only now did she realize just how deeply her feelings for Leigh ran. It was far more than great sex and it had been for a long time now.

The thought of being without Leigh felt worse than being shot, but Morgan had to put Leigh's safety above anything else. Leigh had almost died because of Morgan's feelings for her. Morgan had to take a step back.

She would never forgive herself if something happened to Leigh because of her. No matter how much it hurt her heart, she needed to put Leigh's safety first.

10

LEIGH

"Morgan?" Leigh mumbled. She felt around in bed, but Morgan wasn't there. The bed was strange, too—smaller than it should be.

"The bodyguard is waiting outside the door, where she belongs. Do you remember where you are?"

Leigh's heart sank as the memories came back to her. "In the hospital."

"That's right." Amanda looked up at her from over her iPad. "The surgery to remove the bullet went well. I'm flying in the best rehab specialists as we speak. You won't have any lasting damage; I will make sure of it."

"Thank you, Mom." Leigh knew it was a bad

idea, knew it would look suspicious, but she had to know. "Is Morgan alright? Why isn't she here?"

"I sent her to stand guard outside the door. It's not appropriate for her to be here when you're practically naked."

The flimsy hospital gown Leigh was in certainly didn't cover much, but it was nothing Morgan hadn't seen before—nothing she wasn't intimately acquainted with. Of course, Leigh couldn't say that.

"I see. Have the police been informed?"

"They have. They're going over the crime scene at the house as we speak. Jake is talking to them. How are you feeling? Are you in pain?"

"Just a little. I think they have me on some pretty good painkillers. Mostly I feel tired."

"Well, I'll let you rest in a bit, but first, we need to talk, Leigh."

Amanda fixed her with a steely gaze that never promised anything good.

Leigh gulped. "What is it?"

"I've requested a different bodyguard for you. Her company has excellent reviews, but this particular guard isn't a good fit."

"How can you say that? She just saved my life!"

"I've been watching her. I don't like the way she

looks at you. I think she has impure intentions toward you."

Leigh's breath caught in her throat. She decided to play dumb. "I don't know what you're talking about."

"You know very well what I'm talking about, Leigh. You are not ignorant to the sins of this world. I think she might be a.... *lesbian*... Tell me you haven't seen it."

"I haven't seen it," Leigh lied. "She's just my bodyguard, nothing more."

She had never been a good liar, so it was unsurprising that she wasn't able to convince Amanda of her truthfulness now.

"You need to get rid of her."

"No, I don't! She saved me. I'm not firing her."

"I think there's more to it. I think you have impure intentions toward her."

"How can you say that? I'm engaged to Jake!"

"And I've never seen the two of you so much as kiss!" Amanda shot back.

"So we're not into PDA, sue us! I love Jake." That much, at least, was true. She loved Jake as a dear friend and had for many years.

"If you truly have no feelings for this...

woman... then you'll do as I say and fire her. I will leave you to think on it, and on your future."

Amanda left, leaving Leigh feeling like she was in a cold wind.

How could things have gone so wrong so quickly? Amanda wanting Morgan fired for incompetence was one thing. That was an easy enough charge to foil. Morgan was very good at her job and that wasn't difficult to prove.

Amanda claiming Morgan had *impure intentions* toward Leigh was much trickier, because Leigh was certain that Morgan's intentions toward her were indeed far from pure.

Worst of all, if she didn't do it, Leigh would be in danger of being discovered. She didn't miss the veiled threat Amanda had left her with. Think about your future. If she did anything that even hinted at gay, she would be disowned.

Leigh wanted to scream. It was all happening too fast. She hadn't put anything in place yet. She was supposed to have years to study and make herself employable before being forced into a position where she had to come out to her mother.

It slowly dawned on her. With mounting horror, Leigh realized what she needed to do. If she was going to protect herself and Jake, she would have to break things off with Morgan. Once Morgan was no longer guarding her, she would have no excuse to spend time with her.

Amanda would never accept a "friendship" between the two of them. They would have to break up for real.

Leigh felt tears sliding down her cheeks. The idea of being without Morgan felt like a punch to the gut. She had known for a while now that she was falling in love with Morgan, but she thought that some part of her had always known it was never meant to be.

True happiness had never been a reality for Leigh. These last few weeks with Morgan had been like a dream—the most pleasant dream Leigh could ever have imagined for herself—but it had to end. Leigh had to come back to reality. She had to go back to guarding her secret, to protecting herself.

How the hell was she going to convince Morgan? Morgan wouldn't give up easily. She would fight tooth and nail for them, to give them a chance, but Leigh had to persuade her to give up, somehow.

The door opened and Leigh fought back a grimace as Morgan walked in. Up until a few minutes ago, she had been longing to see Morgan, but now, she wished only to delay the inevitable for a bit longer.

"How are you feeling?"

"I've been better."

"Leigh, I'm so sorry. This is all my fault."

"No, it's not, Morgan. Please, don't blame yourself."

She could tell Morgan wasn't taking her words to heart, but Leigh didn't know how to convince her. She steeled herself to do what she knew she had to.

"Morgan, my mother knows. Or at least, she suspects. She wants you out of my life. I-I have to do it. If I don't, she'll know for sure, and I'll be disowned. We can't... we can't be together anymore." Leigh swallowed a sob on the last word, forcing herself to look into Morgan's eyes.

"I understand."

"What?"

"I understand. I agree, it's for the best."

What the fuck? Hurt and betrayal fanned out through Leigh's chest. She had been so sure that Morgan would fight for her. She had been anticipating arguing for hours just to make even an inch of progress in convincing Morgan that breaking up was the right move here.

And Morgan was just... accepting it?

Leigh took a deep breath, struggling not to cry. "You'll send someone else from your company to protect me?"

"I've already sent the request. I'm just waiting for them to arrive. When they do, I'll go back to your place and collect my stuff."

There was something very wrong with Morgan's face and voice. She didn't sound like herself. Leigh didn't know what was wrong with her, but she was too hurt to pry further. "Fine. Please, leave me, then."

She didn't want to cry in front of Morgan, not now. "As you wish."

Leigh hated how tense things suddenly were between them. Just a few hours ago, being with Morgan had been as easy as breathing, but now, Leigh found she didn't know what to say to her.

Morgan left, closing the door softly behind herself. Leigh knew she was standing guard just outside the door, but that was little comfort. Morgan might as well be on another planet.

When the door opened again, it was Jake.

Leigh held out her good arm pitifully and Jake

immediately pulled her a firm but gentle embrace. "What's wrong, sweetheart?"

"It's Morgan." Leigh lost her battle against tears. "She—we broke up."

"What? Why?"

"It's Mom. She suspects something is between us. I knew I had to break up with Morgan, but I didn't think she'd just agree! I thought she'd fight for me." Leigh sniffed and swiped at the tears running down her cheeks. "I thought she felt the same, but maybe I was never more than sex to her."

"Don't say that. I saw the way she looked at you. Trust me, it wasn't just sex."

"Then why wouldn't she fight for me?"

"Maybe she was just trying to make it easier for you. She had to know what a tough decision this was for you, and she probably just didn't want to make it any harder."

Leigh supposed that made sense, but she still couldn't help but feel betrayed at how easily Morgan had given up on everything they had. Of course, that was ridiculous, given that Leigh was the one breaking up with Morgan in the first place, but she wasn't in the mood to think logically at the moment.

Why did her mother have to be so observant? Things were going just fine before Amanda decided to interfere. Leigh thought longingly of the late mornings spent in bed with Morgan, and the nights they spent talking endlessly after exhausting themselves pleasuring each other.

Leigh loved her. The realization would have taken her to her knees had she not already been in a hospital bed. She loved Morgan, and now she had lost her. The tears came harder and harder until she could barely breathe.

When the nurse came in to give her more painkillers, Leigh took them gladly, allowing sleep to engulf her, hoping it would take away her misery, but her misery followed her into her dreams.

Leigh was released from the hospital two days later. In that time, Morgan's company had sent her another bodyguard. Luke was both professional and friendly. Leigh couldn't find anything about him to object to... except he wasn't Morgan.

She found herself ready to snap at him on a number of occasions for no reason at all other than he did minor things differently to how Morgan did. Leigh knew logically that it made no difference whether he swept the room from left to right, or right to left like Morgan usually did, but it irked her simply because it was a stark reminder of the fact that Morgan was gone.

Leigh received another death threat, but honestly, at this point, she was in so much pain over losing Morgan that she didn't have the emotional energy to be worried about a stalker as well.

When she got home from the hospital, she locked herself in her room, curled up under a thick pile of blankets and cried. She cried for a solid five hours and emerged for dinner with her face blotchy and her eyes so puffy that they were little more than slits.

Jake sat close to her, squeezing her hand every now and then but not trying to force her into conversation, for which she was grateful. Leigh wasn't ready to talk yet. She didn't know if she'd ever be ready to talk. Morgan's absence was like a raw wound inside her, and she didn't think that such a hurt would ever truly heal.

Days stretched into weeks. Leigh barely got out of bed. She had little interest in food, and only showered and changed her clothes out of consideration for Jake.

Three weeks since she had been released from

hospital, Jake came to perch on the end of Leigh's bed. Leigh didn't like his expression. Jake seldom looked as serious as he did now, and it didn't bode well.

"What's wrong, Jake?"

"You know what's wrong, Leigh. You've barely gotten out of bed since you got home from the hospital. You're depressed. I think you should see someone."

"What would I tell Amanda about that? Sorry, Mom, I'm depressed because I lost the love of my life, who just so happens to be a woman, and now I need medical attention for the issue. I don't think that would go down well."

"You don't need to tell her. You get a monthly allowance from your trust fund, and it's not like she keeps tabs on your account."

"That we know of," Leigh muttered. She'd never met anyone more controlling or suspicious than her mother.

"That we know of," Jake agreed. "If she finds out about the appointments, we'll have to make some excuse, but I really think you should at leave give it a try."

Leigh sighed. Just the thought of organizing all that was exhausting. Why bother when she could be eating ice cream in bed and watching crappy reruns on TV?

"I don't know, Jake. I'm not sure that's really necessary."

"Leigh, please just trust me on this. You're not seeing clearly right now. You need help."

"I need Morgan!" Leigh snapped. "But sometimes we can't get what we need, okay, Jake? So maybe you should just leave me alone."

She immediately felt bad for snapping and felt even worse when Jake simply nodded and retreated, murmuring that he would bring her some dinner on a tray later. This wasn't Jake's fault and losing her temper with him only made her feel even worse than she already did.

Leigh checked her phone for what must be the dozenth time today, but there was still nothing from Morgan, not that she'd held out high hopes to begin with.

Jake was right, though. She needed to pull herself together. Leigh had chosen this life—a life of safety without love. Now, she had to live with the consequences. Though it was the last thing she wanted to do, she dragged herself out of bed. She couldn't keep spending every day in bed.

Walking around the garden tired her far more

than it should have given how little time she actually spent moving versus sitting on various benches, but Leigh had to admit that the fresh air did lift her spirits somewhat.

When she got back inside, she opened up her neglected email and wearily started going through messages. There were a lot of them and answering them was the last thing Leigh felt like doing, but she had to do *something*. She needed to get her life back on track.

The rest of her life without Morgan stretched long and empty before her. It wasn't an appealing picture, but it was the picture she had chosen.

Even if she changed her mind now and decided to risk being disowned and not being able to support herself, it was too late. Morgan probably hated her by now, or at the very least looked down on her for her cowardice.

Morgan was brave and always fought for what she believed in. How could she ever love someone like Leigh, who spent her whole life running from the truth, hiding who she was simply because it was the safer option?

Tears started tracking down her cheeks, but this was such a common occurrence nowadays that Leigh barely even noticed. She kept responding to emails, even agreeing to go to a couple of upcoming events.

Maybe getting out of the house would help get her out of her funk. She didn't want to have to see a doctor, but if she didn't manage to pull herself out of this, she might have to. Leigh groaned and rested her head in her hands.

When did the simple task of living become so difficult?

That was an easy question to answer. Ever since Morgan had left, the color had been leached out of life, leaving behind nothing but pain and struggle.

It was what Leigh had to work with, though, so she would just have to deal with it. The wound of Morgan's absence may never heal, but she had to keep going with her life. She couldn't just give up. That's certainly not what Morgan would do, so it's not what Leigh was going to do either.

She could only hope that one day, it would come to hurt less.

11

MORGAN

Morgan existed. To say she lived would be overstating things. Without Leigh, life didn't feel like life anymore. It was just a dreary existence that dragged on and on and on.

She had taken some leave. Thankfully, she had some built up, having never felt the need to be on leave before now. Every morning, she dragged herself out of bed and to the gym to train. She needed to keep her skills and fitness up.

Once she was done with training, she retired to the couch and spent the rest of the day watching sitcoms and crying, more often than not with a big tub of ice cream. By the time evening came, her eyes were sore and puffy, so much that Morgan had invested in special eye drops that the concerned pharmacist had recommended when she had described the problem.

Then, the next day started, and it all began again. Morgan dwelled endlessly on her time with Leigh. It felt like a bright spot in her life, and now that that brightness was gone, everything else was pale by comparison.

She had found the love of her life, only to lose her. Morgan knew it was for the best that they had mutually agreed to break up, but some small part of her had been hoping that Leigh would ask her to stay.

If Leigh had asked it of her, Morgan wasn't sure she could have refused. She could never deny Leigh anything.

But Leigh hadn't asked to her stay, so Morgan had left. Now, it was too late. Leigh had probably moved on by now. Her and Jake's wedding date was drawing ever closer. Soon, they would be bound forever. Leigh would probably take secret lovers, of course.

Morgan considered being one of those lovers, if Leigh would accept her, but the thought left a bitter taste in her mouth. That wasn't what she wanted, for herself or for Leigh. She didn't want a life of hiding who she was like a shameful secret. Morgan was proud of who she was, and she couldn't imagine going her whole life pretending otherwise.

She jumped as her phone rang. Morgan snatched it up immediately, her heart pounding in her throat. It could be Leigh. What if Leigh had changed her mind?

It wasn't Leigh. It was Gray.

Morgan technically didn't have to answer. She was on leave, after all. She didn't really want to talk to anyone, but she answered anyway. Gray was more than just her boss. Over the months of working together, they had become friends as well, and Morgan knew that cutting her friends out of her life just after a bad breakup was a recipe for a downward spiral.

Not that she wasn't in a downward spiral already, but she certainly didn't need to make it worse.

"Hi, Gray."

"Hey, Morgan. How are you doing?"

"I'm fine, thanks, and yourself?"

"No, that's not why I'm calling. I don't want to exchange pleasantries. I want to know how you're really doing. I haven't heard anything from you in three weeks. Did something happen on the last job? You've never taken leave for this long before. If you just need the rest, that's absolutely alright, but I just wanted to check in on you, because I'm getting the impression that there's something wrong."

Morgan sighed. Gray had always been perceptive. It was one of the things that made her so good at her job. She didn't really want to talk about Leigh, but maybe she should. Perhaps sharing the burden with someone else would make it easier to bear.

"I messed up, Gray. I... I fell in love with my client."

"*Oh.* Well, I know all about that. Tell me what happened."

So, Morgan told her. She told Gray everything except details of her and Leigh's sex life. Gray listened attentively, asking only a few short questions, mostly letting Morgan talk. When Morgan was done, Gray was silent for a few moments before speaking.

"Well, you've certainly gotten yourself into a pickle."

Despite everything, Morgan laughed. "Yeah, you could say that. So, what do I do?"

"You fight," Gray said simply. "You don't give up on the woman you love."

"But she doesn't want me."

"Yes, she does. Judging by everything you've told me, she does. She'd just afraid. You need to show her that you're willing to fight for her, that you'll be there for her no matter what. Only when she knows that you're all in will she feel safe enough to take a chance on you."

"You earn enough to support two people, with a few lifestyle changes. Leigh is smart enough to get a scholarship to college. You could make it work. Leigh just needs to trust that you'll be there for her, and to convince her of that after all these weeks of silence, you'll need some kind of grand gesture."

A grand gesture. Could Gray be right? If she showed that she would fight for Leigh, would Leigh truly choose Morgan over the life of safety she had clung to ever since she knew she was a lesbian?

"Are you sure it'll work?"

Gray laughed. "Of course I'm not sure. That's the thing about love—you've got to take a risk. It may pay off, or you may get your heart broken even more than it is now. You need to decide what's most important to you, Morgan. Is Leigh worth risking rejection for?"

That was a stupid question. Leigh was worth every risk it was possible to take. The only question left was what gesture would be grand enough to make up for Morgan neglecting to fight for her in the first place?

Morgan smiled as an idea came to her. There was really only one thing to do.

Despite being dressed for the part, Morgan felt out of place at the charity ball. If all went well, she wouldn't be here for long. She wasn't here to socialize. She was here to win Leigh's heart... Or have hers shattered into a thousand tiny pieces.

Morgan looked around the room, searching faces. Was Leigh here yet? Jake had assured her that she would be. He didn't know what Morgan planned to do, but he had promised to keep Morgan's inquiry from Leigh. Morgan wanted to sweep Leigh off her feet, and she wanted to do so out of nowhere, when Leigh least expected it.

There. Leigh looked resplendent in a dress of shimmering gold, just like Jake had told her. Her red hair was pinned up with loose curls around her face. Morgan fingered the cuffs of her red and gold suit. Her nerves mounted, pinning her to the floor.

Amanda was there, right next to Leigh. Of course, Morgan had known that Amanda was going to be here, but actually seeing her didn't do anything to settle Morgan's nerves.

She had to do it now, before she lost her nerve. Morgan forced her numb feet to move. She reached into her pocket, pulling out the red velvet box.

The sea of guests shifted and Leigh caught sight of her. Her mouth fell open, a million questions in her eyes as she watched Morgan approach.

Morgan ignored everyone around her, focusing only on Leigh. She dropped to one knee and opened the box, revealing a sparkling diamond ring.

She looked directly into Leigh's eyes.

"Leigh Rayson, you are the love of my life. I want to fall asleep with you every night and wake up with you every morning for the rest of my life. I want to stand beside you through thick and through thin. I swear, I will never desert you, and I will always fight for you. I love you, Leigh.

Would you do me the great honor of being my wife?"

Morgan couldn't read Leigh's expression. The guests around them were shocked into silence, but Morgan didn't care about anyone except Leigh. The silence stretched on and on for what felt like hours, though Morgan knew it couldn't have been more than a few seconds.

When Leigh spoke, her voice was loud and clear enough for all the surrounding guests to hear.

"Yes." She beamed at Morgan, incandescent with joy. "I love you too, Morgan. Of course, I'll marry you."

She held out her hand and Morgan slipped the ring onto her finger. Leigh reached down to help Morgan to her feet, and the two of them kissed.

The kiss was both a greeting and a promise, a start of their future together. Elation and joy pounded through Morgan's veins as the guests around them broke into applause.

"What the hell is this! Leigh, this behavior is disgusting! What does your fiancé have to say about this?"

Amanda grabbed Jake's arm and pulled him forward. Morgan's insides twisted. She had always known how Amanda would react, but she wasn't sure about Jake. She knew that this would seriously compromise his own cover. He could be furious with both her and Leigh.

That worry was short-lived.

Jake stepped forward and pulled Leigh into a hug. "Good for you, Leigh. I wish you and Morgan all the happiness in the world."

Morgan had to fight back a laugh at the look of utter horror on Amanda's face.

"Don't think you'll get away with this abominable behavior! Consider your trust fund officially revoked."

Leigh stiffened, but Morgan squeezed her hand. "We're a team, remember. I'm not going to let you starve. I can support both of us until you get a job. We'll figure it out."

Then, something happened that Morgan hadn't accounted for. A woman about Amanda's age she didn't recognize stepped forward. She squeezed Leigh's shoulder and gave her a fond smile.

"Consider my trust fund at your disposal until you get on your feet, Leigh."

Leigh's eyes widened. "Truly, Ruth?"

"Truly, my dear. Your bravery tonight has been

inspiring. The least I can do is offer you a little assistance in setting up your new life."

"Count me in on that," another guest spoke up. "I've got a couple of apartments that I don't use. You're welcome to stay in any of them, rent free, for as long as you need."

A younger man stepped forward. "I work in a job placement agency. I'd be happy to give you a free assessment, Leigh. We can see where your talents lie, and what path would be the best for you to take."

"I know someone in wedding planning who can probably get you crazy discounts on a wedding venue, if you'd like."

Morgan's throat was tight, and Leigh's eyes were brimming with tears. "Thank you," Leigh choked out. "Thank you, all of you. You don't know what this means to me. I swear, I won't waste the opportunities you're giving me. I'll create a new life for myself with Morgan, a life where we don't have to hide."

Amanda was practically apoplectic with rage. Morgan worried for a moment that she might be about to have a stroke. Her face was bright red and she looked ready to explode. She seemed to be teetering on the edge of screaming at Leigh, but half the room was already glaring at her, and she decided to make a strategic retreat. She turned on her heel and stormed out.

Leigh stared after her, her expression unreadable.

"Are you alright?" Morgan asked her quietly.

"Yes. Yes," Leigh repeated with more certainty. "I knew she wouldn't accept me. What I have is exactly what I need, and more than I could ever have hoped for." She leaned in and captured Morgan's lips in a sweet kiss. "I love you."

"I love you too, Leigh."

Morgan couldn't believe it was over. She had known coming in that there was a high chance Leigh would turn her down. Instead, she had everything she could ever have wanted.

"What do you say we get out of here?"

"Yeah," Leigh breathed. "We can go home. Or... Actually, I guess I don't have a home, now. My mother owns my house, legally."

"You have a home with me," Morgan promised. "And from the sounds of it, we'll soon be upgrading, if we take that kind offer that was given to us earlier."

Leigh grinned. "I wish someone had snapped a shot of her face. It was priceless."

"That it was. It—"

Morgan didn't know what it was that alerted her. Maybe it was an errant sound or a sudden movement, or perhaps it was simply her instincts, but from one moment to the next, she knew that something was deadly wrong.

She grabbed Leigh and pulled her to the ground just in time. A bullet went shooting over their heads, hitting the wall behind them.

"Stay down!" Morgan shouted to Leigh. She was up and running at once, darting through the panicked crowd. This time, Leigh's stalker wasn't going to get away from her.

It seemed he hadn't gotten the memo that Leigh was no longer with Jake, which made sense, given that he had been lurking outside the event rather than inside where all the excitement had been happening.

Morgan saw a dark shape and the silhouette of a gun. She threw herself to the side just in time to avoid another shot. She didn't stop moving forward, rolling over the ground and back to her feet, popping up right in front of her attacker.

He yelped in alarm and stumbled back. As his grip on his gun automatically loosened, Morgan wrenched it out of his hands and hit him hard on the side of the head with the handle.

Leigh's stalker dropped like a stone.

Morgan took off her tie and used it to bind his hands before grabbing him by the ankles and dragging him back to where she had left Leigh. No way was she going to risk letting him out of her sight until the police had arrived.

Leigh was standing by the venue door, along with a crowd of others. Jake gasped when he saw who Leigh was dragging.

"That's Simon!"

"You know him?"

"We dated—it has to be ten years ago now. I barely even remembered him. *He's* who has been stalking Leigh? Why now, after all this time?"

"That's for the police to figure out. There was probably some recent trigger in his life, a stressor that made him long for a past stable relationship. He fixated on you, but since you weren't available, his obsession switched to taking Leigh out of the picture. We can't know for sure until he's questioned, but whatever his reasons, at least he won't be on the loose anymore."

"I'm not so sure." Leigh bit her lip. "It's not like

I have access to money to hire the best prosecution lawyers anymore. What if he gets off?"

"He's not going to." Yet another guest stepped forward. "My brother is an attorney specializing in criminal law. He's one of the best, and I'm sure I can convince him to take your case pro-bono."

Morgan supposed she shouldn't really be surprised by such generosity coming from people attending a charity gala, but it still took her breath away how many people were willing to support Leigh.

If Amanda had crushed Morgan's faith in people, it was being renewed tenfold right here and now. She put an arm around Leigh as Leigh stammered her thanks. Someone had already called the police and there were sirens sounding in the distance.

Morgan took a deep, settling breath. It was truly over now.

Now, she and Leigh had nothing to do but plan the rest of their lives together.

EPILOGUE

Four years later
Leigh

L eigh shifted slightly, looking through the line of her peers, trying to spot her wife. There she was. Morgan was right next to Jake and Mike, who were holding hands. A mere three weeks after Leigh and Morgan had gotten engaged, Jake had come out to his family.

He told Leigh that she inspired him, and they walked each other down the aisle at one another's weddings.

Neither of them had had any contact with their

families since coming out. It was sad, but Leigh had learned to live with it. Jake and Mike had their own little family now—two beautiful twin girls, less than a year old.

Morgan waved at Leigh, her eyes shining with pride. Leigh waved back, fingering her graduation robes, making sure they were hanging right. She was graduating top of her class in computer programming and already had a number of companies vying to have her work for them, who were happy to have her part time while she finished her postgrad.

The dean started calling names. Leigh was near the end, which gave time for her nerves to mount. Not that there was any reason to be nervous. She had already earned her degree, after all; all she needed to do now was accept it.

Still, she was nervous, and she sought Morgan's gaze again. Morgan gave her a warm, reassuring smile and a thumbs up. Leigh took a deep breath just as her name was called and stepped forward to receive her degree.

Everyone cheered and threw their hats when it was over. Morgan was the first one to reach Leigh, and the two of them kissed right there in front of everyone. No one paid any attention to them; they were all too busy celebrating with their own families.

Even after four years, it still sometimes blew Leigh's mind that she could love Morgan freely and openly. After living with her mother's hatred and condemnation all her life, she had begun to think that everyone must feel that way, but that wasn't true.

Sure, they had encountered their share of homophobia, but most people were decent.

They already had their celebration plans set; their table booked at Leigh's favorite restaurant. Leigh felt a small twinge of regret that her mother couldn't be here, but she was quickly distracted from those thoughts by Morgan's mouth near her ear, whispering how proud she was of her. Morgan pressed a few kisses to Leigh's neck, drawing a soft sigh from Leigh.

Morgan and Leigh ate and drank late into the night. Jake and Mike had to excuse themselves early, as they only had the twins' babysitter until eight. By the time they got home, Leigh was pleasantly tipsy and more than a little horny.

She grabbed Morgan by the shirt the moment they were inside and hauled her up against a wall, kissing her fiercely. Morgan returned the kiss in kind, flipping them around so that Leigh was the one pressed against the wall, a position Leigh didn't object to in the slightest.

"Let's make a baby," Leigh breathed.

Morgan pulled back. "Are you drunk? We can't make a baby, sweetheart. I don't have the equipment for it."

"Yes, we can," Leigh insisted. "With doctors and science and stuff, we can. They can take our DNA and use it to fertilize eggs or something like that. I'm sure I read about it somewhere..." She trailed off, aware that she had just branched into potentially perilous territory. She and Morgan both wanted children, they had discussed that already, but there was a difference between wanting them as a theoretical concept versus wanting them *now*.

She needn't have worried. Morgan's expression softened. "I'd love to make a baby with you, Leigh. We'll wait to hear what you say when you're slightly more sober, though. If you still want this tomorrow, I'm all in. Though might I suggest you get settled in your new job before taking on parenthood?"

Even in her buzzed state, Leigh was able to see the merit of that suggestion. She nodded, giving

Morgan a silly grin. "What would I do without you?"

"We're never going to have to find out," Morgan promised. "Now, will you let me take you to bed?"

"Always."

Morgan lifted Leigh up and carried her bridal-style through to the bedroom. Leigh giggled as Morgan laid her gently on the bed and started undressing her. Leigh squirmed back and forth, helping Morgan remove her dress then her underwear. Finally, she was naked before her wife.

Morgan took her own clothes off quickly before joining Leigh on the bed. They kissed again, slow and soft and deep. Morgan's hands trailed down, finding Leigh's nipples and squeezing hard.

Leigh gasped as she instantly felt her pussy moistening rapidly. That move never failed to get her wet and Morgan knew it.

Leigh whimpered and spread her legs in invitation, but Morgan wasn't going to let her off that easily. Morgan reached into the bedstand and got out the set of padded hand and ankle cuffs that she had bought Leigh for their last anniversary.

Leigh moaned at the sight of them, squirming as her pussy and clit throbbed, aching for attention. She spread herself on the bed, allowing Morgan to attach the cuffs to the hooks they had installed in the bed frame.

Once she was tied, Leigh started tugging on the restraints, finding it as satisfying as always to struggle lightly against them and be reacquainted with just how little give they had.

She was so busy testing the bindings that she didn't notice what Morgan was doing until Morgan started licking her clit.

"Ah—fuck! Morgan, please, baby. You promised."

"I did promise, didn't I? You've been so good."

"I have," Leigh practically sobbed. It had been three weeks since she'd been allowed to come. Every day of those three weeks, Morgan had licked her clit until she was a writhing quivering mess, right on the edge of orgasm, but stopping just before tipping her over the edge. Morgan knew Leigh's limits very well by now and never failed to use that knowledge to her advantage.

She had promised Leigh that she could come after graduation, and Leigh was desperate to collect on that promise.

"I don't know. You know we have a rule about sex when drunk..."

"I'm not drunk!" Leigh wailed. "I'm tipsy, that's all, I swear!"

Morgan chuckled, stroking a hand down Leigh's face. "I know, baby. I'm just teasing you. Don't worry, you'll get to come... but only when I say so."

Morgan went back to licking Leigh, bracing herself on one elbow and using her free hand to play with Leigh's nipples.

"Harder, please," Leigh breathed. "Morgan, fuck, I'm so close already."

Morgan hummed an acknowledgement, and the delicious vibrations sent through Leigh's body almost tipped her over the edge.

"Stop!"

Morgan pulled back just in time, leaving Leigh tensed and panting, desperately trying not to come before it was time.

Morgan grinned. "Good girl. Lie back and relax for me."

Leigh did as she was told, following Morgan with her eyes. Morgan got out Leigh's favorite vibrating egg and a strap-on clit vibrator. Leigh had some idea of what was coming, and she was practically quivering in anticipation.

Morgan turned the toys on and put the one

inside Leigh, where it slid in easily, given how soaked Leigh's pussy was. Leigh lifted her ass so that Morgan could strap the clit vibrator on. She cried out as Morgan turned it on, the strong vibrations almost too much for her.

"Morgan—fuck! I'm going to come!"

"No, you're not. You're going to hold on until you've gotten me off. Then, and only then, can you come."

Leigh moaned in despair, sure that she was going to fall short. "Hurry, then. I don't know how much longer I can last."

Morgan grinned wickedly as she gave one of Leigh's nipples a hard twist, which had Leigh crying out, her body surging even as she frantically tried to think non-sexy thoughts.

It was difficult to do that when her sexy wife was climbing onto her face, positioning herself so that her clit was perfectly aligned with Leigh's tongue.

Leigh started licking, long and hard, interspaced with small, lighter licks, just the way she knew Morgan liked it.

She usually liked to take her time, bringing Morgan to the edge slowly, but tonight, she had no patience for such games. She put her all into it, and soon had Morgan rocking onto her tongue and chanting Leigh's name.

Morgan clutched the headboard as she came, grinding down onto Leigh's face so hard that Leigh could scarcely breathe, but Leigh didn't care. All she cared about right now was the perfect noises Morgan was making, noises she drank in and could never seem to get enough of, no matter how many times her wife came on her tongue.

Morgan pulled back, her face flushed as she caught her breath. "How are you doing, baby?"

"I need to come," Leigh whined. "I'm so close, Morgan, please..."

"Alright. You've been so good for me. You can come, Leigh." As she spoke, Morgan put her hand directly on the clit vibrator and pushed it firmly downward, right on top of Leigh's clit.

Leigh screamed as she came, her pussy contracting so hard that it pushed out the egg vibrator, but she was barely aware of that. She was squirting all over the bed and crying out Morgan's name as she came in hot bursts that never seemed to end. She was consumed with an unending wave of pleasure that threatened never to release her.

When it finally ended, it left Leigh limp and breathless. She was barely aware of Morgan untying her and pulling her close. Leigh snuggled happily into Morgan's arms, pressing a soft kiss to her cheek. "I love you."

"I love you too, Leigh. More than anything."

Leigh was on the point of drifting off when she remembered. She groaned, wondering if it was worth doing this when she was so peaceful and happy.

"What's wrong?"

"I got an email from my mother. It came in just before I was about to go out with everyone else to graduate, so I didn't get a chance to look at it. I'm not sure I want to. Maybe I should just delete it."

Leigh hadn't heard from Amanda in four years, and she wasn't sure she wanted to speak to her again, not when speaking to her would undoubtedly involve a lecture on how disgusting and unacceptable her behavior was.

"Do you want me to read it first and make the call?"

"Yes, please," Leigh said in a small voice.

Morgan took her phone and opened the email. A smile unfurled on her face as she read. "You'll definitely want to read this. I promise, it's not going to ruin your mood."

Well now there was no way Leigh could

decline to read the thing. She took the phone from Morgan and read.

Dear Leigh

Over the past four years, I have had a lot of time to think — about your choices, and about mine. I have missed you, and in the last year and a half, I've begun to wonder if it is worth clinging to my beliefs if they are constantly going to drive us apart.

So, I started doing some research into the LGBT+ community. I've spoken to people in a number of queer-friendly forums and even made friends with a few of them!

Leigh, I was wrong. I am so sorry, sweetheart. I never should have made you feel as though you are less because you are gay. I accept you, and I would love to meet up with you and your wife for coffee sometime, if you are willing.

I understand if you are not willing to mend old fences, but if you miss me as I miss you, then I hope you will respond.

. . .

Yours Always

    Mom

Leigh only realized she was crying when a tear dropped onto the phone. She brought her eyes up to meet Morgan's. "I can't believe it. Of all the people—I never guessed she might change her mind."

"Me neither," Morgan admitted. "I guess it just goes to show that miracles are possible. Do you think you'll meet with her?"

Leigh hesitated. "I don't want her money. I'm sure she'll offer me my trust fund back, but I don't want to be dependent on her like that again. I don't trust her enough for that."

"That's fair. We have our own lives now. You've already got those three very good job offers. We don't need her money. We're doing just fine."

"That being said, I think... I think I'd like to meet with her. If there's any way I can have her in my life—and have her accept me—I want to try to make it happen. I'll only do it if you agree, though. Her choices have hurt you, too. If you say no, we'll pretend like this email never happened."

"Leigh, of course I agree. She's your mother—

and my mother-in-law. I want us to have a relationship with her if that's possible."

Leigh found herself grinning so widely it hurt her face. "Then I'll respond. Maybe we can meet up sometime this week."

"That would be wonderful." Morgan leaned in and kissed her forehead. "The perfect end to a perfect day."

It truly was. When she woke up this morning, Leigh had had everything she wanted, and somehow, tonight she was going to bed with much more. Tonight, she had the promise of family, both her old family and a new one with Morgan.

She wondered how Amanda would react to the news that she would be getting grandchildren. Surely, she'd be happy. When Leigh and Jake were engaged, Amanda was always dropping hints about them conceiving sooner rather than later once they were married.

"What are you thinking?"

Leigh snuggled closer into Morgan. "I'm just thinking about how happy I am. I love you so much, it's difficult to describe."

"You don't need to describe it—you show me every day." Morgan tightened her arms around Leigh. "I hope that I show you the same."

"You do. It's in the way you touch me, the way you smile, the way your eyes twinkle when you look at me. Every day, I know I am loved."

"And you will be for every day to come," Morgan promised.

Leigh didn't doubt her for a moment.

ALSO BY EMILY HAYES

If you enjoyed this one, I think you will love the next book in the Bodyguard Series, check it out below!

When the politician disagrees with her bodyguard, she can't control the sparks that are flying between them

This is an Age Gap, Enemies to Lovers, Coming Out, Bodyguard Romance. It is super steamy and as always a

Happy Ever After.

Elizabeth Myers is a politician passionate about LGBT rights.

When her personal safety is threatened she knows she needs a bodyguard.

She immediately disagrees with her new ex military bodyguard Alex Jameson who is just trying to ensure her safety. The chemistry between them is heated.

When lines become crossed between them, Elizabeth knows that it needs to be kept secret for the sake of her career- she isn't ready to come out yet.

But will their secret fling ever really be enough for either of them? And will secrets ever really stay secret?

mybook.to/Bodyguard3

VIP READERS LIST

Hey! Thank you so much for reading my book. I am honestly so very grateful to you for your support. I really hope you enjoyed it.

If you enjoyed it, I would love you to join my VIP readers list and be the first to know about freebies, new releases, price drops and special free *hot* short stories featuring the characters from my books.

You can get a FREE copy of Her Boss by joining my VIP readers list : https://BookHip.com/MNVVPBP

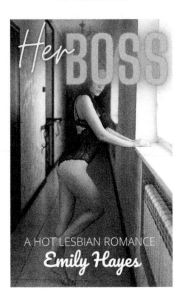

Meg has had a crush on her hot older boss the whole time she has worked for her. Could it be that the fantasies aren't just in Meg's head? https://BookHip.com/MNVVPBP

Printed in Great Britain
by Amazon

27841475R00099